FALLEN ANGEL

JOHN LING

Nothing fixes a thing so intensely in the memory as the wish to forget it.

Michel de Montaigne

PART ONE

1

Auckland isn't Baghdad.

That's what Kendra Shaw told herself as she sat in a café on Queen Street, back pressed against the wall, sipping on an ice-cold mocha.

All around her, the lunchtime crowd was buzzing. The air smelled of sweat and perfume.

Kendra tried to relax, tried to be normal.

But so far, it wasn't working.

Outside, past the windows, cars were stopping at the intersection for the red light, gleaming under the summer sun. And… she just couldn't help herself. Eyes darting, she scanned each individual vehicle, studying their suspensions, front and rear. She tried to decide if any of them are sinking under excessive weight.

She calculated the odds, felt her muscles coiling up, her heart thudding in her ears and…

No.

Kendra twitched, catching herself before the adrenaline dump washed over her. Jaw pinched, face hot, she forced herself to breathe.

In through the nose.

One, two, three.

Out through the mouth.

One, two, three.

Slowly, surely, her pulse slowed, and the tension melted away into a tingle. Hunching over the table, she ran her hand through her hair and stared down at her drink.

No, Auckland isn't Baghdad, and you're not going to find any car bombs here, no matter how hard you look.

Kendra curled her lip.

Her therapist had warned her about this – the dangers of negative thinking. Sure, the pills would help, but their effectiveness only stretched so far. If she failed to get a grip, she would only aggravate her condition. Maybe descend into full-blown neurosis.

Only think happy, positive thoughts. You're back home now. Stop obsessing about operational security. That's in the past. That's not your life anymore.

Kendra sucked up the rest of her drink, her straw screeching.

Auckland isn't Baghdad.

She repeated it over and over like a mantra, internalising it. And she decided that, yeah, she was going to go for walk around town. A simple, pleasant walk. Which meant no craning her neck to search for snipers, no dodging alleys to avoid choke points, and of course, no agitating about passing vehicles.

What was it that her therapist had said?

Psychological reconditioning.

Hell, yeah. She needed to tweak her expectations and erase her preconceptions. Untangle her doubts. And maybe – *just maybe* – if she rewired her brain enough, she'd stop being so afraid of shadows that weren't there.

Damn straight.

Pushing back her chair, Kendra stood up, angling for the café's exit.

And that's when she saw him.

2

Ryan Hosseini.

That moment of moments was like a million pinpricks on her soul. Searing. Red-hot. And she felt everything at once.

Longing.

Anger.

Regret.

There he was on the sidewalk outside the café, wearing a suit, clutching a briefcase, gliding through the crowd. And – *damn it* – he still had that hitch in his step; that tightness in his shoulders; that posture of loneliness that he carried everywhere with him like an eternal burden.

Ten years.

Ten *fucking* years.

And nothing had changed.

As Ryan faded from her line of sight, Kendra blinked hard. Not knowing what to think.

Twist of fate.

Cosmic joke.

Karma.

Whatever.

Somehow, in a city this big, their trajectories had collided, atom to atom. And – *oh God* – she was snivelling, her throat raw.

Stay away from him. He doesn't need you in his life. And you don't need him in yours. Not after all that's been said and done.

But – *no* – another part of her wanted to rebel against that logic. She wanted to believe that maybe – *just maybe* – this was an omen. A sign. A chance.

Ten years. Goddamn it.

Kendra forced herself to breathe.

In through the nose.

One, two, three.

Out through the mouth.

One, two, three.

And she made a decision.

Do it. Just do it.

Stabbing her nails into her palms, Kendra stepped out of the café, sweat beading her forehead. She plunged into the crowd, trying to catch up to Ryan.

And that's when she saw them.

3

A three-man surveillance crew.

Classic ABC structure.

The first man – Alpha – was directly behind Ryan, matching the tempo of his movements. The second – Bravo – was several paces behind Alpha, occupying the rearguard position. And the third – Charlie – was just across the street, covering the widest possible angle.

The technique they were using was known as the rabbit and the eye. In this case, Ryan was the rabbit, Alpha was the eye, and the rest of the team were the chasers who followed the eye.

Their formation was smooth, assured, continuously adjusting for variations, no matter how minor.

Collectively, Kendra had picked them right out of the crowd because of the way they were built – broad shoulders that tapered down to slim hips. That telltale physique that only special operators had.

Kendra also noted the way they were dressed. They wore untucked shirts and cargo trousers, along with tactical boots. At first glance, their fashion was casual, but to her practised eyes, it marked them as being dangerous. Loose-fitting clothes with plenty of pockets meant room for weapons and ammunition, and their choice of rugged footwear indicated that they were ready for some serious action.

Who are these guys? And why the hell are they shadowing Ryan?

The pit of Kendra's stomach burned with the familiar rise of adrenaline, and her skin bristled.

But she forced herself to breathe.

Breathe.

She loosened her steps, relaxed her posture and drifted into the thickest part of the crowd, acquiring cover and concealment.

Kendra swallowed.

Cover and concealment...

She was surprised at how easily she had slipped into that frame of mind. But – *damn it* – this was a shadow parade worthy of Hitchcock.

Coincidence? Or correlation?

That's when Kendra remembered Jim Braddock's words, coming at her like a subliminal message, a gravelly whisper from the past.

Little girl, operators never do anything by chance. Never. And that's why we study the black arts, don't we? So that we can trump the odds in favour of precision.

Kendra puffed her cheeks.

Right…

She had to assume that this op was being choreographed according to someone's script, someone's timeline.

But whose, though? And what's the endgame here?

Ahead, Ryan had stopped at an intersection, waiting for the crosswalk signal to turn green. Pedestrians pooled around him, and just behind, Alpha and Bravo held their positions. Charlie provided support from across the street, lingering right at the edge of the kerb, his head swivelling.

Playing it safe, Kendra turned away. She pretended to study a jewellery shop's display, and she used the window's reflective surface to check on Ryan.

While she was too far back to make out his face, she could tell that he was anxious. He was constantly shifting his weight from one foot to the other and fidgeting with his briefcase. He didn't appear to be surveillance conscious. Or, if he was, he wasn't showing it.

For fuck's sake, Ryan. What have you gotten yourself into?

Kendra tousled her hair, frustrated.

The crosswalk signal turned green with a chime, and pedestrians from all four corners surged on to the street, zigzagging, and the surveillance crew exploited that very moment to swap roles within the crowd.

Alpha dropped back to Bravo's position.

Bravo switched up with Charlie.

And Charlie took up point directly behind Ryan.

Smooth. Very smooth.

Breathing through her teeth, Kendra watched Ryan make a beeline for the Farmers department store on the corner of Queen and Victoria.

4

The automatic doors parted, and Ryan hesitated, just for an instant, before bowing his head and slipping inside.

Charlie followed, and so did Alpha.

Bravo hung back, taking a seat on a bench across the street.

Kendra narrowed her eyes. Her first impulse was to close in and reacquire Ryan. But, no, that would have been the wrong move.

Bravo had a clear view of the store's entrance, and she had to assume that he was in constant communication with Charlie and Alpha. She couldn't possibly trip his radar without provoking some kind of reaction.

Also, the store acted as a choke point. Sure, she was familiar with the layout of its aisles. Farmers sold everything from clothes to cosmetics to homeware. But if she stepped inside now, she would only be funnelling herself into a restricted environment with very little room to manoeuvre.

Finally, she still didn't know what the hell was happening here. Was this a surveillance-detection run? Or was a brush pass about to take place? Or a dead drop?

There were just too many damn variables.

So Kendra made a snap decision. She turned and retraced her steps, moving away from Bravo's line of sight.

She got out her phone and started dialling. She desperately wanted to reach her former boss at Section One, Deirdre Raines. But she only got through the first four digits before she stopped. She scrunched up her face and shook her head ever so slightly.

Get real. Deirdre's going to think you belong in the loony bin.

And that, unfortunately, was the truth.

If Kendra told Deirdre what she was seeing, then the Ice Queen would simply chalk it up to a hallucination and send men to yank her off the street immediately. And by the time Kendra worked through the bureaucratic loop and convinced them that she wasn't delirious, the opportunity would have been lost.

Ryan...

Kendra bunched up her shoulders.

She decided that she needed something more solid.

So she took a left turn at the junction ahead, carrying on, taking yet another left turn at the next corner, and she made a complete pass around the block. Now she was coming in from the opposite direction; ahead of the store; ahead of Bravo.

Jaw clenched, she spotted a lull in the traffic and cut across the street. Getting out her phone, keeping it at waist level, she took rapid-fire shots of Bravo using the camera. And she darted into the mouth of an alley directly opposite.

She waited.

The sight lines were clean.

She had good coverage of both Bravo and the store's entrance.

Perfect.

She still didn't know what the hell was happening in there. But once Ryan and the two other operators, Charlie and Alpha, stepped back outside, she would be able to photograph all the players and, if possible, supplement that with video.

And then…?

Well, then Deirdre would have to pay attention. Something serious was clearly happening here, and Kendra was the best person to intervene before it reached its natural conclusion—

And that's when a searing flash came from the store, blinding as a second sun, and the windows rippled and blew out in a crescendo of fire and glass.

Kendra lurched and pinballed off the wall behind her, hitting the ground, her nostrils scorched, her eyes watering.

5

Kendra had a memory.

It was a wistful memory, creeping up from the cobwebs of the past.

...*She was sitting on a children's swing, breathing in the smell of freshly cut grass, and he was behind her, pushing her harder, higher, and she squealed and laughed, gripping the rattling chains, her knuckles white, her feet damn near touching the sky...*

They were both teenagers back then, much too old to be horsing around like that. But it didn't matter. Nothing mattered. Because it was summer, and they had each other.

Kendra blinked, and the vision was gone, dissolving like ash. She coughed and wheezed, her cheek flat against the pavement. Her mouth felt dry, shrivelled up, and her ears were humming.

Everything sounded distant, hollow.

People were yelling.

Tyres were screeching.

Alarms rang out.

Muscles taut and shivering, Kendra groaned. She rolled on to her side, then her back. She cupped her face with her hands. Her skin felt raw, tingling like electricity, and she shook her head from side to side.

Slowly, very slowly, the throbbing and nausea eased.

Jaw clenched, she staggered to her feet. She felt her joints creak and pop, and she listed this way and that before she found her bearings. She steadied herself against a lamp post, and rubbing her eyes, she peered past dust and tears, and everything came into focus.

The Farmers store was on fire, and the air was thick with smoke and ash and swirling embers. Traffic had piled up all along the street, and stunned bystanders intermingled with bloodied survivors.

It was chaos, absolute chaos.

Kendra jostled through the crowd, skipping over grit and rubble, craning her neck, panting, searching. But the blaze was too strong, too blinding, and there was no way anyone within the kill zone itself could have survived.

Ryan...

Her stomach churned with grief and rage and confusion, and she felt like crying, like screaming. But − *no, no* − she swallowed back the urge and forced herself to breathe. *To breathe.*

Doubling back, Kendra found Bravo still at the bench directly opposite the store. Only... his posture was all wrong. He was sagging back, drooping halfway off his seat.

When she got closer, she saw why.

A jagged shard of glass had stabbed him right through the neck. He had a white-knuckled grip on it, and blood was fountaining through his fingers, and he sounded like he was retching, choking.

Fuck.

Kendra wrapped her hands over his, applying as much pressure on the wound as she could, being careful to keep the glass immobile. 'Hey. *Hey.* Can you hear me? Who are you? What kind of op were you running?'

All the man gave her was a pale and vacant stare. His grip on the glass was weakening.

Kendra used her knee to nudge him. 'Come on. *Stay with me.* Why were you tailing Ryan Hosseini? *Why?*'

The man convulsed, retching harder. Spit bubbled on his lips, and with a final exhale, he went slack. His eyes rolled back, and he slid off the bench completely and crumpled against the ground, like a damn marionette puppet whose strings had been severed.

Frustrated, Kendra checked the man's pulse. She confirmed his vital signs were nil, and she dabbed her hands against his shirt, wiping the blood off, and she proceeded to pat him down.

She found a smartphone. A wallet. A car key attached to a fob. A holstered pistol accompanied by a sound suppressor and ammo. And, finally, a tactical-folding knife.

Kendra didn't have time to ponder the significance of what she had uncovered. Curious onlookers were already gathering around her, rubbernecking, murmuring.

Bending over, she used her body to hide the sight of the weapons from them. She clipped the knife on the inside of her hip pocket and secured the gun under her waistband, between her navel and her appendix. Then she stuffed the rest of the items into her other pockets.

Coolly, calmly, she rose and stepped away.

'Oh my God,' a woman gasped. 'Is he dead? Please tell me he's not dead.'

Kendra ignored the woman and pushed past.

And – *shit* – that's when she froze.

A man on a motorcycle was accelerating around the intersection ahead, needling his way between gridlocked cars, heading southbound on Queen Street.

The man's face was hidden behind his helmet.

But Kendra recognised his clothing, his posture...

Ryan.

6

Adrenaline seared her senses, and Kendra broke into a flat-out run, cutting across the intersection.

She dodged an arriving fire engine, then an ambulance, and they blasted their horns. She lurched and recovered her footing, mouth gulping air, muscles stretched to burning point.

Ryan was gaining speed, pulling away from her – *fifty metres, eighty metres, hundred metres* – and she yelled – *Ryan, Ryan* – but the motorcycle's engine was shrieking like a banshee, drowning her out, and all she could do was watch as he melted away at the next intersection.

Finally, Kendra stopped running, and she doubled over, hands on her knees, bile clawing at the back of her throat. She started to shake, feeling dizzy, anguished. betrayed.

This was a goddamn set-up. Ryan isn't the victim here. He never was.

7

Kendra looked back and saw that first responders were already establishing a perimeter around Farmers.

They were drawing up barricades and shepherding people out of the red zone.

With her heart hammering in her ears, her emotions churning, Kendra blended into the crowd. She moved past the civic centre, past Aotea Square, past the town hall.

She covered three blocks, then she peeled away from the crowd and stepped into a public restroom.

Kendra checked that it was empty before cleaning herself up. She washed away the blood and grime and dust. She finger-combed her hair, then she locked herself inside one of the stalls.

Sitting down on the toilet, she cradled her head in her hands. She coaxed herself to breathe.

In through the nose.

One, two, three.

Out through the mouth.

One, two, three.

Straightening, hands on her cheeks, she listened to the shouts and sirens echoing from outside. It was a terrible symphony, and the gravity of the situation sank in.

Here she was, a washed-up agent caught up in a terror strike apparently perpetrated by an old boyfriend.

Fuck. Fuck. Fuckity-fuck.

Kendra didn't want to believe that this was happening.

And yet... she couldn't deny the obvious.

Ten years is a long time. Ryan could have changed. He could have been radicalised.

She felt a surge of guilt in her heart, stinging like acid.

By choosing to serve – *by choosing to leave* – had she hurt him that much? Had she pushed him in the wrong direction? Was she ultimately responsible?

Kendra groaned and slammed her foot against the wall beside her. Damn it, she wasn't sure if this was love or obligation or just madness. But there was no turning back now; no return to innocence.

Get a grip. Get a fucking grip. And work with what you have.

Kendra inhaled and exhaled.

She replayed the sequence of events in her mind. She picked everything apart, moment by moment, and she remembered the briefcase that Ryan had been carrying. She remembered how uncomfortable he had looked with it.

Was that the bomb?

But, no, that wasn't possible.

The sheer force of the blast, coupled with the scale of the damage, suggested a larger device. One packed with an incendiary like thermite or phosphorous, and that would have been too bulky to fit into a briefcase.

Which meant that the actual bomb was already hidden within the Farmers store, maybe inside a storeroom, wired to detonate beforehand.

Kendra had to assume that Ryan must have ditched the two operators, Alpha and Charlie, by slipping out the back of the store, leaving them to be caught in the blast. Vaporised.

But why?

Kendra swallowed, and she got out the wallet she had taken from the dead operator, Bravo. She thumbed through it. According to his driver's licence, his name was Thomas Cronin, and he lived on the North Shore. And according to his business card, he worked for an investment firm, also on the North Shore.

A bullshit proposition.

Kendra knew all too well that pocket litter like this was seldom, if ever, the real thing. They only existed to solidify a legend; a cover identity.

Next, she took a look at Mr Cronin's smartphone. She checked the data and call logs. And... everything was blank. Which meant that it had been set to self-erase.

Kendra figured it must have been Mr Cronin's final act before he died.

She popped out the phone's battery, along with the SIM and memory cards. Right now, she didn't want anyone tracking her position.

Better to be paranoid than sorry.

Tilting her head, Kendra unholstered the pistol. It was a Heckler & Koch. She released the magazine and performed a press-check on the gun before racking the slide and catching the ejected round. A forty-five. Subsonic.

She worked the slide a few more times and found the action to be smooth, well-oiled.

Professional maintenance.

Kendra reloaded the gun and fitted the sound suppressor on to the muzzle. It snapped on with a click. Seamless. Completely unlike traditional suppressors, which had to be screwed on.

Custom-made. Match-grade.

Kendra removed the suppressor and holstered the gun.

Then she drew the tactical-folding knife. It was an Emerson. She thumbed open the blade. It was non-reflective black, partially serrated with a spear point. Flexing her fingers around its moulded grip, she carved lines through the air – seven o'clock and three o'clock – before folding the blade shut.

Slick. Very slick.

The fact that Mr Cronin was kitted out with subsonic rounds, a custom suppressor and a tactical folder meant that he was prepped for some serious wetwork.

But why?

Biting her lip, Kendra got out Mr Cronin's car key. She narrowed her eyes. It had no logo, no emblem, no identifying marks of any kind. But, still, she considered the possibilities.

8

When Kendra stepped out of the washroom, she saw a police helicopter hovering above the skyline.

Her muscles tensed up, but she reminded herself that the authorities weren't going to lock down the entire city centre.

At least not yet.

Their standard-operating procedure called for a policy of containment. They would focus on extinguishing the blaze, triaging the wounded and moving civilians out of the red zone. They wouldn't be looking to detain anyone at this point, or canvass the wider area.

Which means that I still have some time.

Kendra made her way to a multi-storey parking garage two blocks down. She had worked out the distance, measured the odds, and she had decided that this was the best possible candidate.

It offered the quickest access to three motorways – the North, North-Western and Southern – and it was also tactically close to Farmers, presumably the focal point of the op.

Kendra approached the parking garage from the rear. There were five levels. She hazarded a guess and used the stairs to reach the basement level.

Vehicles of every make and model flanked her.

Eyes darting, she began the process of elimination.

She ruled out bright colours like yellow and red. They were too flashy; too conspicuous. And she also excluded midrange colours like white and metallic. Still memorable. Which only left hushed tones like grey or black. They were surveillance friendly; able to blend in without attracting attention.

Next, Kendra crossed off any vehicle that was too big or too small. Which meant no SUVs. No vans. No hatchbacks. No sports cars. And that only left the sedans, which offered the perfect mix of mass, acceleration and a low centre of gravity.

Finally, Kendra rejected the sedans that were parked front-first into the bays. She only zeroed in on those that were reverse-parked. This was common sense. Mr Cronin and his team would have wanted a no-fuss exit. Just get into the car, start the engine and pull away. No clumsy manoeuvres.

With all the options whittled down to a minimum, Kendra approached a grey Toyota Camry and aimed the car-key fob at it, depressing the button.

No joy.

She moved on and tried a black Holden Commodore.

This time, the car chirped and flashed and unlocked.

Bingo.

Kendra looked past the windscreen at the prepaid parking ticket displayed on the dashboard. She saw that it was due to expire in an hour, and she found that very revealing.

Thomas Cronin and his buddies didn't plan on sticking around for very long. This was meant to be a milk run. Touch and go. No fuss. Only... it didn't work out that way.

Smirking, Kendra was tempted to get into the car right now.

But, no, she had to be smart about this. Meticulous.

Stooping to a crouch, she duck-walked around the Holden. She fingered the underside of the bumpers, probed behind the tyres and peered at the undercarriage.

Kendra did this inch by inch.

She orbited the car twice.

And so far, so good.

But she wasn't done.

Not yet.

Kendra flicked out her knife and – *slowly, very slowly* – she opened one of the doors just a fraction. She slid her blade all along the gap between the door and the car's frame, back and forth, top to bottom. She only opened the door completely once she had confirmed that there was no tripwire present.

Kendra repeated the process for the remaining doors.

She cleared them the exact same way.

Next, she moved on to examining the car's interior. She only reached in with her upper body, careful not to lean against the seats until she had examined every crevice, every groove and every corner with light from her phone. Just to be sure that no pressure switches had been installed.

That done, Kendra moved to the back of the Holden. She used the car key to unlock the trunk, but kept her palm firmly on the lid to prevent it from springing up. She raised it carefully, using her knife to clear the gap before opening it completely.

The interior looked empty, but when she rolled back the mat and shifted the spare tyre, that's when things got interesting – there was a backpack hidden underneath.

Kendra tugged it out and checked the pockets. Spare ammunition. Surveillance gear. Night-vision goggles. A laser-aiming module. And an infiltration kit.

An operator's idea of Christmas.

When she unzipped the top of the backpack, she saw that the fabric extended over the wearer's head and folded over the chest and stomach, becoming a ballistic vest. Wraparound design, good protection, easy access to the pockets.

Christmas and New Year's.

Refolding and zipping up the bag, Kendra slung it across her shoulder and closed the trunk.

She moved to the front of the Holden. Popping open the hood, she inspected the engine. She aimed her light this way and that. She detected nothing suspicious, and she shut the hood.

Sighing, Kendra finally allowed herself to sit down on the driver's side. She pulled open the glove compartment. She confirmed that it wasn't wired, and she found a GPS navigation unit inside. Turning it on, she tapped the screen and launched the list of recent destinations.

Kendra swallowed, recognising the one at the very top.

It was an address in Remuera.

Ryan's parents.

9

Kendra closed her eyes and remembered.

...She was meeting his parents for the first time, and she saw the coldness in their eyes, felt the weight of their judgement, and she realised right there and then that she was an outsider – the wrong skin colour, the wrong social status – and her knees went weak, and her heart pounded, but he was brave, so brave, clutching her hand tight, standing tall, telling them that she was his girlfriend...

Kendra opened her eyes. She blinked hard and sagged against the steering wheel. She felt as if a fat cat was sitting on her, overpowering her ability to think, to rationalise.

Shaking her head, she straightened. It would have been all too easy to key the ignition and get going, but she decided not to.

Sure, the Holden didn't appear to be booby-trapped. But that didn't mean that a tracker hadn't been hardwired into the car's electronics. And even if there was no tracker, stealing the car was still a bad idea. Traffic in the immediate area was bogged down. She wouldn't be going anywhere in a hurry.

So Kendra placed the GPS unit back into the glove compartment and stepped out of the Holden and locked it with a *chup-chup*.

She didn't have to worry about leaving any prints behind. The pads of her fingers had been chemically scrubbed years ago. One of the many procedures done to turn her into a ghost while operating in foreign countries.

Irony of ironies. What works abroad works just as well on home soil. Who would have thought?

Kendra felt a stab of bitterness for what she had become; for how much things had changed.

She turned and started to walk away from the Holden, making for the stairs. And that's when she heard the telltale clap of a suppressed pistol, and she felt a sharp hiss just above her right shoulder, like a bumblebee had just zapped past, parting her hair.

Kendra flinched, and her heart seized up.

Fucking hell…

Someone had just taken a shot at her.

10

Kendra ducked and scrambled for the safety of the closest car.

Gasping, panting, she crouched right behind the engine block, knowing that this was the most solid part of the vehicle, offering the best protection.

Two more rounds ricocheted off the car's hood, drawing sparks from the bodywork.

Huddling against the car's tyre, Kendra reached behind her and unzipped the top of the backpack. She pulled the ballistic vest down over her head and secured it around her front. Then, drawing her pistol, she snapped the suppressor on.

Despite the adrenaline, she forced herself to take measured breaths and slow her racing heartbeat. She didn't want to get anxious and over-pressurise her blood with stress. She couldn't afford fidgety muscles and frantic thoughts.

Breathe. Focus. Stay calm.

Kendra peered under the car, trying to locate the tango, but the view was too limited, and she couldn't see a damn thing. However, she didn't want to raise her head above the hood either, nor did she want to make herself visible through the car's windows. That's exactly what the tango would be expecting.

So Kendra crab-walked to the rear of the car instead, taking up a new position right beside the trunk. Of course, this was a risk. The trunk was the weakest part of any vehicle, its hollow construction making it easy for bullets to pass through. But she was counting on her vest to protect her, and besides, she didn't plan on sticking here for too long.

Kendra inched sideways, curving herself around the rear bumper, tracking her gun this way and that way. The fact that the tango was using a suppressed weapon made it difficult to determine where he was, but she figured that he had descended from the staircase, so she aimed in that general direction—

That's when another two rounds drummed into the front of the car, this time shattering one of the headlights, sending fragments of plastic and glass tinkling.

Kendra inhaled.

He still thinks I'm right beside the engine block. He's trying to keep me pinned down so he can outflank me.

Kendra exhaled, feeling her confidence rise.

He didn't have an exact fix on her position, and that was good.

She heard footsteps echoing, and she craned her neck. She caught a glimpse of the tango. He was threading his way between the vehicles up ahead, his pistol raised in a two-handed grip, his body held sideways in a Centre Axis Relock stance, minimising his profile.

He had broad shoulders that tapered down to slim hips. And, yeah, he wore an untucked shirt with cargo trousers.

He's part of the surveillance team. The fourth member. Delta.

That realisation didn't give Kendra much comfort.

Somehow she had missed him earlier, and the only way that could have happened was if he was on overwatch duty, perched high on a rooftop, helping his team at street level with optics.

But she decided not to agonise over it.

Doesn't matter. All that counts is right here, right now.

Kendra leaned out, taking aim at Delta, acquiring a sight picture.

She knew her posture wasn't great and the angle was poor, but she fired a cluster of shots anyway, puncturing the windows of one car, then another.

Their alarms went off, wailing in a shrill tempo, and Delta reacted by zigzagging backwards and dropping out of sight.

Kendra knew she hadn't hit him, but that wasn't the point. She only needed to halt his forward momentum so that she could make a move.

Rising to one knee, she fired several more shots, then she turned and launched herself into a dash, keeping her head down, reaching the row of vehicles just opposite.

She slid into cover behind the closest car, flattening herself behind the engine block just as Delta fired on her once more. Bullets thwacked into the car's front grill and ripped into the tyres. Air whispered from the shredded rubber as the car sagged.

Sweating, Kendra sucked in breaths through her clenched teeth. She performed a tactical reload, swapping her half-empty magazine for a full one.

She wondered if anyone would respond to the alarms.

Maybe the police?

Maybe private security?

Hell, no...

Everyone was too preoccupied with the blast at Farmers.

Who would care about a little ruckus happening in a parking garage?

Shaking her head, swallowing, Kendra made a quick assessment of her situation. Delta was blocking her path to the stairs, so that route was definitely out of the question. However, there was a ramp right behind her. It led up to the next level.

If only I can get to it...

Kendra decided that some dialogue with Delta was in order, if only to buy herself some time. So she cleared her throat and raised her voice over the sound of the alarms, 'Hey! Listen! I didn't kill your team down at Farmers. I had nothing to do with that.'

She waited.

She counted down the seconds.

Eventually Delta spoke, his voice angry, his accent local, 'You're lying. I saw you frisking Cronin. That's how you got the keys to the car. You're working with Onyx.'

Kendra used the distraction to peel away from the car she was using as cover, and she carefully inched her way around the next car behind her. 'Onyx? Is that the code name you've assigned to Ryan Hosseini?'

'Don't fuck with me. You know exactly who Onyx is.'

Kendra inched past yet another car. 'No, I don't know. I was only trying to help your friend. He was hurt real bad—'

'Shut up! Just shut up!'

Kendra heard running footsteps, followed by Delta firing his weapon in a wild barrage. He was striking the car that he thought she was still hiding behind. Then Kendra heard the metallic echo of his pistol's slide locking back on empty.

That surprised her.

Delta had given in to emotion, and now he had left himself exposed, running dry on ammo at the worst possible moment.

Exploit it. Now.

Kendra abandoned her plan to go for the ramp. Instead she went on the offensive. She button-hooked out of cover, bringing her pistol up to bear, sidestepping, and she caught Delta leaning against a minivan.

He was dropping his spent magazine and about to slot a fresh one in.

She jerked her chin, closing the distance. 'Drop it. *Drop it.*'

Delta's face was contorted in rage, and he slapped his magazine in anyway, releasing his gun's slide and chambering a round.

Kendra double-tapped him in the chest.

He staggered back, grunting, bumping against the minivan's side mirror. He fell to one knee, but he still managed to raise his weapon, his aim wobbling. He was obviously wearing a ballistic vest under his shirt.

Kendra had no choice.

So she double-tapped Delta in the forehead, and he went down for good.

11

Kendra took shaky breaths as she came down from the adrenaline high. The smell of gunsmoke filled her nostrils, and she felt sick to her stomach.

Goddamn it. I wanted him alive.

She stared at Delta's body. Blood was pooling around his shattered skull, looking almost black against the concrete floor.

I had to do it. I had to. It was either him or me.

Grimacing, Kendra removed the suppressor from her pistol and holstered it, then she stowed away her ballistic vest.

She started patting Delta down, and she found his wallet. The driver's licence said his name was Peter Wong, and just like Thomas Cronin, he worked in an investment firm on the North Shore.

She checked his phone, and as expected, it was blank. Set to self-erase.

She collected his gun, his knife, his ammo. Then, stepping back, she brought her own phone out and took pictures of Wong.

It was gruesome but necessary.

Already, the alarms from the cars had gone silent, cutting off automatically. The garage was quiet as a tomb.

Kendra was tempted to clean up after herself. Remove all the spent shell casings. Mop up the blood. Hide the body. Eliminate as much forensic evidence as possible.

But she didn't have the time, not the inclination.

Fuck it.

Shaking her head, she made for the stairs.

12

By the time Kendra hit the sidewalk, the bells at a nearby church were tolling. When she got closer, she saw frightened people streaming in, looking for refuge, for solace.

She lingered for only a moment before moving on.

She headed west, away from the city centre, towards Ponsonby.

She wanted to put some distance between herself and the red zone, yes, but she also needed to get someplace where the traffic was free-flowing.

As she brisk-walked, Kendra thought back to the GPS navigation unit that she had found in the operators' car.

She thought about Ryan's parents.

What do they have to do with any of this? Are they involved? If so, how much?

She didn't like the implications, and worse still, she couldn't just ring up Deirdre Raines and seek clarification. As defiant as it was – *as irrational as it was* – she didn't want Section One to get involved here. Because they couldn't help her. Not with their *fucking* bureaucracy and rules and duplicity.

Kendra raked her hand through her hair, face pinched.

But... there was one person, at least, she could reach out to.

Getting out her phone, she used it to log into a darknet portal, and from there, into an email account she had set up years ago. It was designed for contingencies just like this one.

Kendra typed out a message to Jim Braddock.

Are they pitching up the circus tent today? Came across four clowns just now, and they didn't look too funny. The acrobat tossing the knives was funny, though.

Kendra included her phone number and attached the photo she had taken of the dead operators, Thomas Cronin and Peter Wong. Then she saved the message as a draft and logged out.

The virtual cut-out was the perfect way to avoid detection. Because nothing was actually transmitted over the wider internet, the chances of interception were slim, and since Kendra was using a prepaid, disposable SIM on her phone, only Jim would be able to call her back. And when he did, he would be savvy enough to use a disposable SIM of his own.

Any contact between them would be off the radar.

Jim had been out of the service a long time, but he still had the inside juice on covert ops, and if there were rumblings on the circuit, he would know about it.

Kendra had faith that her mentor would give her a straight-up answer.

Still, she wasn't sticking around to wait for his reply.

There wasn't time.

She reached the New World supermarket at Freemans Bay. She skirted around it, and finally – *finally* – the streets ahead looked open and clear.

She flagged down a passing taxi. 'Remuera, please.'

13

When the taxi driver pulled away from the kerb, he jerked his chin at the pillar of smoke blackening the sky. '*Damn*. Will you look at that? They're saying it's a gas-leak explosion. A construction crew dug up the wrong spot. Cut into a pipeline.'

Sitting in the back seat, Kendra met his eyes in the rear-view mirror. She gave him a non-committal shrug. 'I was just passing through when they blocked off Queen Street. Didn't get the chance to see much of anything.'

'Yeah, well, it sounds bad. Real bad.'

Kendra stretched her lips thin. 'Mm-hm.'

'You're lucky that I picked you up when I did. My dispatcher's been bugging me to quit my fares in the inner city. With all that gas floating around, it's just too dangerous.'

'Yeah, too dangerous.'

The taxi driver smacked the steering wheel. 'It's the government and all their cost-cutting. They're screwing around with our infrastructure and putting all of us at risk. I'm telling you, I'm voting them out the next time around. You ought to do the same.'

'For sure.' Kendra nodded politely, tuning out as he continued to vent.

They hit the motorway.

Kendra got out her phone and logged into the New Zealand Herald website. And, sure enough, the Farmers explosion was breaking news. Only, just like the taxi driver said, it wasn't being reported as an act of terror.

Kendra furrowed her eyebrows.

They're making it sound accidental. Unintended. And why would they do that unless they're trying to cover up a counterterrorism op gone bad?

She could only guess which alphabet-soup agency was involved.

SIS? GCSB? NBCI?

Flexing her jaw, Kendra logged out of the Herald and into Google Maps. She zoomed in on Remuera. She panned back and forth over the topography, studying the lay of the land.

She couldn't shake the feeling that something was waiting for her there.

Something ugly.

Inhaling, exhaling, Kendra thought back to what her therapist had said.

Avoid alcohol.

Avoid drugs.

Avoid emotional attachments.

Yeah, her therapist had warned her about the dangers of placing herself in a situation where she could lose control, because once the tipping point was reached, she could very well suffer another breakdown. A permanent one. And when that happened, Section One would have no choice but to commit her to the loony bin.

But – *hell* – here she was, doing exactly that. She was risking her sanity, her freedom and her life for a slippery descent into the heart of darkness.

Kendra leaned back against her seat and tried to rein in her emotions.

She could only hope that she was doing the right thing.

Whatever that was.

PART TWO

14

Remuera was a leafy suburb dotted with genteel mansions and rolling slopes and ocean views. It was prosperous, exclusive, picture-perfect.

Kendra had the taxi driver drop her off several streets down from the actual address, and she hit the sidewalk, breathing in the smell of sea salt as she performed a slow sweep of the neighbourhood.

She observed fashionable young mothers pushing their infants along in designer prams, well-groomed retirees sipping tea at upscale cafes, and yachts bobbing in the sun-kissed waters of the bay close by.

The mood was relaxed.

Almost too relaxed.

Shaking her head, Kendra realised that this place was a bubble wrapped within a bubble, where folks didn't believe that the troubles of the world could touch them. Part of it was entitlement, and the other part of it was naiveté. And if the powers-that-be said that the blast in the city centre was an accident, well, they would buy it.

But Kendra knew better because she had seen the shadow of the beast, tasted a trace of its venom, and she wasn't about to be lulled into a false sense of security.

She quickened her steps. She zigzagged from one side of the street to the other, then she backtracked.

Eyes darting, she searched for signs of surveillance. She checked for pedestrians who tried to echo her movements or tried to look as if they weren't. And she inspected the vehicles around her – parked or passing. She checked to see if any had tinted windows, because tinted windows were a dead giveaway for covert observers.

Kendra moved in an elliptical loop.

She scanned far and near.

Nothing tripped her sixth sense.

Stretching her shoulders, Kendra adjusted the straps on her backpack. She felt secure enough to zero in on the address. So she moved off the sidewalk and stepped on to a cobbled pathway, entering a park.

Trees flanked her on either side, branches forming a canopy that swayed and swooshed overhead, penetrated only by shafts of sunlight. Stray leaves crackled under her shoes. Birds twittered.

It was idyllic.

Soon Kendra encountered a fork in the path, and without thinking, she chose to go right. And that led her straight into a recreational area, where children were playing on slides and swings and mazes, shrieking and laughing.

Kendra stared, and – *damn* – that's when the melancholy hit her, like a talon scraping across her heart.

This was the place – *the exact same place* – that Ryan and her used to hang out.

Back when they were happy.

Back when they were innocent.

Before everything got fucked up beyond recognition.

Lips trembling, Kendra forced herself to turn away. Retracing her steps, she returned to the fork in the path and opted to go left this time.

It occurred to her why her subconscious had led her in the other direction to begin with. It was born out of a desire to revisit the pain, to punish herself. Because young love was fleeting, all too easily lost like tears in the rain.

Kendra dug her nails into her palms, cheeks twitching.

Focus. Focus on the objective. That's the only thing that matters right now.

She took measured breaths.

Keep calm and carry on.

Soon Kendra reached the other end of the park, and she found a good vantage point – a bench positioned in a secluded alcove ringed by bushes. And Ryan's parents' home was just downhill, two-hundred metres away.

Sitting down, Kendra reached into her backpack.

She got out the monocular that was part of the surveillance gear.

Pressing it against her right eye, she aimed it downrange. The image was hazy at first, but then the lens whirred and automatically adjusted, and the mansion came into focus.

Yes, the place was just as she remembered it.

Lush.

Grandiose.

Imposing.

Kendra swept her gaze over the perfectly manicured gardens, the tennis court, the swimming pool.

No movement.

No threats.

So Kendra scanned the windows of the mansion itself. Left to right, top to bottom. And... it was strange. All the blinds and drapes were pulled tight. Every single one. There were no gaps to peek through. Not even a sliver.

Kendra inspected the rooftop, and she saw that the rollers on the skylights were shuttered as well.

It didn't make sense.

She thought about Ryan's mother, Leila. She remembered how the woman used to obsess about natural light and had insisted that the mansion be constructed to incorporate it. That was Leila's pride and joy.

So why shut out all the sunshine? Especially on a summer day like this?

Kendra lowered her monocular. She mulled over the contradiction, and tilting her head, she got out her phone and dialled the mansion's number from memory.

The line on the other end rang and rang, but no one picked up.

That felt *very* wrong.

Ryan's father, Saeed, was active in business and philanthropic circles, and he had a reputation for being a perfectionist, a nitpicker. He would never have tolerated a missed call.

Such old-school sensibilities meant that a member of the household staff was always – *always* – on hand to answer the phone. And on the slim chance that no one at all was available, Saeed certainly would have made sure that the answering machine was connected.

Kendra sucked in a breath and hit the redial key on her phone. This time, she allowed the line to ring and ring until it timed out. All she was left with was a dead tone.

Damn it...

Kendra grimaced. She felt the slow burn of adrenaline in her gut. That incendiary mixture of dread and anticipation.

I'm going to have to move in.

15

Refocusing the monocular, Kendra measured the sight lines. She calculated the angles of approach, and she decided that there were two ways to reach the mansion.

The first option would be to descend the slope, turn left and exit the park. That would allow her to converge on the mansion from the front. Obvious enough. But that approach presented a problem – because the property sat at the end of a cul-de-sac, the street leading into it shared a single point of entry and a single point of exit.

Practically speaking, that was less than ideal, because if she did choose to go down that route, she would only be funnelling herself into a choke point. And if she ended up bumping into trouble – *God forbid, an ambush* – she'd have precious little room to manoeuvre.

Kendra shook her head.

Tight. Too damn tight.

Which meant that the second option was better. She would descend the slope, turn right and remain within the confines of the park. Just ahead was a pond, and snaking all around it was a walking track rimmed by tall grass and shrubbery, and directly beyond was the rear of the mansion.

Sure, the route was meandering, indirect, but the terrain was advantageous. It offered multiple directions for her to fall back on in the event of an emergency. And, of course, all the vegetation didn't hurt – they would serve as cover.

And that settles it.

Puffing her cheeks, Kendra shouldered her backpack and moved down the slope.

She angled right.

She hit the walking track.

She observed ducks and geese squawking on the pond, joggers and cyclists making their rounds, and of course, the ubiquitous mothers pushing along their prams.

Kendra was conscious of every person she walked past – their smell, their aura.

Flexing her fingers, she kept her arms close to her sides, ready to go tactical if anyone so much as gave her the wrong signal.

Her muscles tensed up.

Her skin prickled.

And, head swivelling, she closed in on the walls of the mansion.

Fifty metres.

Thirty metres.

Ten metres.

Breathing evenly, keeping her heart rate in check, Kendra peeled away from the walking track. She diverted to the mansion's eastern side and found herself exactly where she needed to be – at the back gate, which led directly to the outhouse.

Huddling against a tree, she reached behind her and unzipped the top of the backpack. She pulled the ballistic vest over her head and secured it around her front. Then she drew her pistol and attached the suppressor.

She took aim at the CCTV camera perched on the wall above the gate and double-tapped it. Sparks flew, and the camera shattered with a dull thump.

Kendra approached the keypad beside the gate. She crinkled her lips. She searched her memory, then nodding, she punched in the security code.

1979.

The year of the Iranian Revolution.

The keypad chimed, and the gate unlocked.

16

Kendra slipped through the gate and moved into the rear courtyard. She sidled up beside the outhouse and assumed a bladed stance, pistol at the low-ready.

She glanced through the windows.

She saw garden tools in storage but nothing else of interest.

Inching along, Kendra peered quickly around the corner of the outhouse – *once, twice* – before slicing past it, pistol at the high-ready.

She moved forward in smooth, deliberate steps, minimising noise, maximising her balance.

Just ahead was the swimming pool, and as she drew closer, she saw twigs and leaves floating on its surface, forming a mucky layer.

That caused her to frown.

Leila and Saeed were absolute sticklers for tidiness. They were prone to micromanaging the affairs of their home, so it didn't make sense that they would have allowed the pool to get clogged up like this.

Kendra shook her head ever so slightly.

She felt a growing sense of unease.

Skirting around deckchairs, she advanced up a marbled pathway, glided past trimmed hedges and flowerbeds in full bloom, and she flattened herself against the glasshouse.

She spotted another camera.

She double-tapped it.

Circling around, Kendra reached the gazebo at the far end of the garden. She crouched and took cover behind one of its arched columns. She flicked her gaze over the windows of the mansion itself.

She had already examined them earlier, but that was done at a distance.

Now that she was closer, she needed to be doubly sure.

So Kendra holstered her pistol on her vest, got out the monocular and performed another security audit.

She took her time. She was searching for windows where a section of the glass had been cut and removed. Because that's what a shooter lying in wait would do. He would keep himself way back from the window, only using the hole in the glass to fire through once he had acquired a target.

So Kendra checked, checked and rechecked.

Just like before, all the windows looked intact. There was no tampering, and more importantly, all the blinds and drapes behind them were drawn tight. There were no convenient gaps that would allow a shooter to discharge his weapon.

Good.

Still, Kendra wasn't ready to move.

She continued scanning. She inspected the rooftop, the surrounding foliage, every possible nook and cranny. And – *damn* – she felt her optimism sinking.

Kendra couldn't deny the obvious – to get to the mansion itself, she'd have to cross over fifty metres of open lawn, and there were multiple positions where a concealed shooter could still take a crack at her if she left the safety of the gazebo.

Cover would be minimal, and the fact that it was broad daylight didn't help.

Lowering the monocular, Kendra brushed sweat away from her forehead.

And even if I do make it that far, what would be the best point of entry? I'm going to need one that won't leave me exposed while I make the breach. A tough one.

And that's when Jim Braddock's gravelly voice echoed in her thoughts, prodding, admonishing.

Little girl, no line of approach is ever a hundred percent. Best you can do is avoid engaging in kinetic action until you have carried out a thorough security audit. And even then, all you'll get is eighty percent. Or sixty. Or forty. So take your pick. They don't call it the fog of war for nothing.

Refocusing the monocular, Kendra began searching for a solution, something to offset the risks, and with renewed zeal, she found it.

The garage at the side of the mansion was sandwiched between the main building and the compound wall. It offered decent cover, and for lack of a better option, it would serve as the best point of entry.

The only problem was she still had to cut across the open lawn to reach the garage, and in doing so, she could very well blunder into a shooter's field of fire.

Tricky. Awfully tricky.

But Kendra had a strategy in mind.

Based on experience, she knew that a moving target was harder to hit than a stationary one, and even harder still was a moving target that happened to be zigzagging in a haphazard way.

So Kendra figured that's what she had to do. Go in hard and fast and keep her line of approach erratic and unpredictable. And hopefully – *hopefully* – that would tip the odds in her favour.

Putting the monocular away, Kendra took slow breaths.

She tightened her stomach, feeling the liquid warmth of adrenaline.

Do it. Just do it.

With a sharp exhale, she launched herself out from behind the gazebo, and with her shoes squeaking on the grass, her vest rustling, she darted at random.

Left, right.

Right, left.

Panting, heart racing, she half-expected to hear the snap of a gunshot, the chomp of a bullet. But – *man, oh man* – she kept her eyes fixed on her goal.

She gritted her teeth. She felt the tendons in her neck straining. And – *oh yeah* – she cleared the lawn and whipped around the side of the garage, skidding to a crouch.

Another camera loomed.

Palms damp, she quick-drew her pistol and shattered it with a double-tap.

17

Kendra took a moment to calm her frayed nerves.

She allowed her breaths to level out.

I'm either real lucky or real paranoid.

She didn't know which was which.

Duck-walking, she peered around the corner ahead. She scanned the long oval driveway, the baroque fountain, the front gates at the far end.

Everything was quiet.

Still.

Too fucking still.

Kendra backtracked, wiping sweat from her chin.

At this point, she would have expected her intrusion into the compound to provoke more of a response, especially after she had taken out multiple cameras. But, so far, there were no boots on the ground. No potshots. Zero pushback.

Maybe nobody's watching. Or... maybe nobody's around.

Kendra groaned and shook her head.

She didn't want to settle on unfounded assumptions.

Holstering her pistol, she reached into a vest pocket. She got out the infiltration kit and unpacked it.

She extended a scanner wand and ran it along the periphery of the garage's side door, and it vibrated when she reached the top right-hand corner, its LED light flashing green.

That meant that the door was fitted with an alarm, but it wasn't active.

Kendra hesitated.

She felt that familiar dash of unease.

Why would the security system be disabled?

Chewing the inside of her cheek, Kendra got out the fibrescope. She snaked the lens under the door and peered through the eyepiece.

The interior of the garage was cloaked in semi-darkness, like a cave.

She panned left and right, up and down. She saw nothing more threatening than a Porsche and a Ferrari, parked side by side. But her angle was limited. She couldn't see beyond those two vehicles.

There was a chance that a shooter could be lying in wait for her.

It was unlikely, but she couldn't rule it out.

Kendra put away the fibrescope and got out the Peterson universal key. She slid it into the keyhole, and with a bump and a jiggle, she got the door unlocked.

Kendra reassembled the infiltration kit and pocketed it. She got out the night-vision goggles, mounted its harness over her head and tightened it. Then, drawing her pistol, she snapped on a laser-aiming module.

It felt strange to be doing this right in the middle of the day, but if all the windows in the mansion were shuttered, then she had to assume that visibility would be patchy. In that case, equipping herself with the goggles would be a win-win.

It would automatically adjust for differentials in light levels, amplifying the contrast when it was gloomy, dimming it when the environment was brighter.

This would allow her to maintain consistent and uninterrupted vision.

Better to be paranoid than sorry.

Kendra positioned herself beside the door and flipped the goggles down over her eyes. She knew she had to be decisive with making the breach because the doorway was a fatal funnel. This was where a shooter could take a crack at her while she was silhouetted against the daylight.

Kendra rolled and stretched her neck.

She swallowed.

And... here we go.

She pushed the door open and slipped through in a button-hook manoeuvre.

She was quick and fluid, and once she was inside, she shut the door behind her, maximising the darkness, maximising her advantage.

Sidestepping, she activated the infrared laser on her gun, visible only to her night-vision, and she performed a slow orbit of the garage.

Her senses were alive, and she picked up on the smallest of details. The faint scent of exhaust and motor oil. The motes of dust shimmering in the air. The slow, careful padding of her footsteps.

Kendra skirted around the Porsche and the Ferrari. She moved past two more vehicles – a Lamborghini and a Mercedes SUV.

And that's when she saw something else in the corner.

A motorcycle.

18

Kendra blinked hard as she approached the motorcycle and touched its engine.

Still warm.

Her breaths grew hitched.

Her chest felt tight.

She couldn't believe it. She didn't want to believe it. So she craned her neck and checked the registration plate. And – *hell* – it matched. This was the exact same motorcycle that Ryan had used to make his getaway.

Nostrils flaring, Kendra took a step back, raking her fingers through her hair. She struggled to process this new revelation.

He's here.

Kendra turned and eyed the door ahead. It led out of the garage, into the house itself. And she just stood there, swaying, agonising.

He blows up a department store and neutralises a team of operators. Then he comes back here to his parents' home. But that doesn't make sense. He should be doing something smart, like skipping town, gaining distance.

Kendra thought back to the GPS navigation unit that she had found in the operators' car. About how it connected to all of this. And... she drew a blank.

The only obvious fact was that Ryan was mixed up in something bad, something god-awful, and Kendra wondered what confronting him would mean.

Can I pull the trigger? Can I afford not to?

Her hand flexed around her gun, and Kendra shook her head, her face pulled tight. She knew that dwelling on the anguish wouldn't help. It would only colour her judgement and give her the jitters. And now, more than ever, she needed to be calm, precise, rational.

So she got her breathing under control.

She reined in her emotions and straightened.

Focus on what's in front of you. Just on what's in front of you. Locate, isolate and contain Ryan. Then maybe, just maybe, you'll get some answers.

Hardening her jaw, Kendra crept to the door.

She didn't like the situation, but at least she had one perk. If Ryan was here, it meant that all the motion detectors in the house were disabled, and she didn't have to worry about tripping any alarms.

Taking bitter comfort in that, Kendra opened the door and stepped through.

19

Kendra found herself at the bottom of a stairwell, and the first thing she noticed was the dip in temperature. The air had become cooler, drier.

It took her a moment, but then she realised why – the air conditioning was purring from the ventilation ducts above, which meant that it was circulating throughout the house.

It was obviously a sign that she wasn't alone.

Kendra mounted the staircase, gun raised, and as she climbed, she kept herself to the side, away from the handrail, shoulder brushing against the wall.

She knew that she was vulnerable to attack from above, so she acquired the widest possible angle, keeping her pace slow and deliberate.

When she reached the landing at the top, she rounded the corner and continued up the next flight of steps. She emerged into a foyer. The smell of perfumed incense filled her nostrils. It was a mixture of rose and apple.

Kendra paused.

A Persian rug lay spread out before her, and oil paintings lined the walls, lush and intricate Iranian landscapes that stood out even under her green-hued vision.

Kendra recognised two of the paintings, but the rest were new. The collection had obviously been updated since the last time she was here.

Kendra felt the stirrings of the past.

The last time I was here, things didn't end up so well.

With her cheeks twitching, she moved on.

She continued down a hallway. She remembered the layout well enough. The music room was on the left. The library was on the right.

Eyebrows furrowed, Kendra chose the music room and button-hooked into it. She swivelled her head from side to side to compensate for the tunnel vision that her goggles gave her.

A grand piano stood at the centre of the room. The walls were adorned with tapestries. The heavy drapes at the windows were pulled shut.

All clear.

Kendra backtracked and slipped into the library.

A computer workstation sat in the corner. Shelves filled with books reached to the ceiling. The blinds at the windows were shuttered.

All clear.

Kendra moved through the study and accessed the door at the far end. It opened out into another hallway.

As she stepped through, that's when she caught the scent of something sharply metallic. It was enough to make her flinch, her mouth puckering up. It was the stench of blood. She'd recognise it anywhere.

With her heart throbbing in her ears, Kendra cleared the hallway and button-hooked into the living room.

The sickly sweet smell got stronger.

She dodged a sprawling sofa set and moved past the supersized television, past a table covered with Persian pottery.

And that's when she saw the bodies.

20

Six bodies.

They were lying face down on the floor, hands bound behind them with flexicuffs, each executed with a single gunshot to the back of the head.

From the way they were positioned, it looked like they'd been forced to kneel before the inevitable slaughter.

God Almighty.

Kendra shifted their heads to check on their faces, and their necks moved easily. Minimal rigor mortis, which meant they had been dead for only a few hours.

She studied the entry wounds. They were small in diameter, and there were no exit wounds. That indicated a .22 calibre. An assassin's weapon.

She scanned the carpet. She looked for spent casings, but she found none. That meant the killer had cleaned up after himself.

God Almighty.

This felt like a bad dream.

The worst possible dream.

Kendra had spent years on the global circuit. Finding, fixing and finishing threats in *souks* and *madrasas* and back alleys. Spilling blood in every *jihadi* stronghold from Baghdad to Kabul to Islamabad.

But nothing – *absolutely nothing* – had prepared her for how she felt right here, right now, because she knew these people.

The driver.

The cook.

The gardener.

The butler.

The maids.

They had served the Hosseini family for years.

Kendra fidgeted. She felt bile clawing at the back of her throat, sticky and hot.

Did Ryan do this?

She stared hard at the bodies, and that's when something else occurred to her. The air conditioning had been switched on specifically to slow the rate of decomposition. And blocking out all the sunlight? It amounted to the same thing.

He wanted to preserve his handiwork. Preserve the scene of the crime.

Kendra knew that there were two kinds of killers.

The first was the psychopath – the one who killed his victims because he thought they deserved it. And the other was the sociopath – the one who killed his victims because he just didn't care.

The way the household staff had been executed was ruthless, expedient, completely devoid of any kind of passion. And that pointed more to a sociopath, not a psychopath.

No, Ryan wouldn't just snuff out the people he grew up with. Not without displaying emotion. It doesn't make any sense.

Yet Kendra found a contradiction with that line of reasoning. The aftermath of the killing indicated some kind of perverse emotion at work; some kind of intimacy.

Why is he trying to preserve the bodies? Is this his way of showing affection? Does it even count as affection?

Kendra hated to admit it, but her knowledge of behavioural profiling was rudimentary at best, and despite her best efforts, she was grasping at straws here.

All she knew was that she had to find Ryan.

She had to lock him down before anyone else got hurt.

21

Kendra swept the rest of the ground floor, corner by corner, room by room.

The cold and the dark and the silence conspired to make her burden worse. Her mouth was dry, her muscles were tight, and her nerves were frayed. But she couldn't afford to seek relief by flicking on a light switch or peeling back a curtain.

All she could do was push forward, probe the shadows, brave her doubts.

Once Kendra was sure that the ground floor was clear, she returned to the middle of the house. She approached the grand central staircase. It was broad and majestic, with handrails made out of carved wood and glossy ivory.

Kendra mounted it backwards, taking each step slowly, carefully.

Above her, the second floor was rimmed by a long balustrade balcony which looked down on the entire staircase, which made it the perfect strike point for an ambush.

Don't rush. Take your time. Do it right.

Kendra aimed her gun this way and that way, her laser puncturing the gloom. She listened to the gentle creak of the steps below her; the steady tick-tock of a grandfather clock close by; the constant purr of the air conditioning.

Head swivelling, Kendra logged in the angles, the lines of sight, the lines of fire. She measured them, ready to react at the slightest flicker of movement, at the smallest sound that didn't belong.

The seconds stretched.

The short hairs on the back of her neck prickled.

Kendra reached the landing that divided the staircase.

Rounding the banister, she took the next flight of steps by climbing forward. But she remained cautious until she crested the top of the staircase itself. And slowly, very slowly, she swept the balcony, employing a technique known as slicing the pie, acquiring the widest possible angle.

All clear.

Kendra paused only to suck in a breath and exhale, then she carried on with her search, corridor by corridor, room by room.

Finally – *finally* – she slipped into the master bedroom itself.

It was tidy and airy, sumptuously decorated in a baroque style.

Her eyes fell on the four-poster bed.

There was paper strewn all over it – pamphlets, booklets.

Frowning, Kendra approached and picked one up, and she blinked, her insides cramping up.

Goddamn...

Her written Farsi was basic, but she knew extremist literature when she saw it.

Jaw clenched, Kendra flicked through the others, and it was all the same. Extolling the virtues of the Supreme Leader. Encouraging global resistance. Calling for the destruction of the West.

22

Trembling, Kendra swept the house a second time.

She was no longer cautious, just moving at a clipped pace, slicing the corners with a vengeance, gripping her gun so tight that her knuckles were white.

And... she found nothing.

Ryan was gone.

Fuck.

She had the faintest sense that she had missed him. Just barely. And she felt like she was drowning in a maelstrom of confusion, caught up in the bubbling froth of a tidal rip that she couldn't control.

It's amazing how someone can shatter your heart, and you can still love them with all the little pieces that you have left.

Kendra stumbled back into the living room, and she found what she was looking for – a console on the wall.

She jabbed a finger at the touchpad, and it chimed, and with a collective hum, all the blinds and curtains in the house rolled back.

Sunshine surged through the windows, chasing away all the shadows.

Kendra tore off her night-vision goggles, and with spots dancing before her eyes, she sank to the floor, her chest heaving. She had never felt more drained, more lost.

This can't be happening. This can't be fucking happening.

She stared at the bodies lying in the corner and shook her head. She had always assumed that Ryan was one of the good guys. Moderate. Liberal. Westernised.

But was she just blindsided by what they had shared?

Was she swayed by psychic wounds?

Damn it.

And that's when she felt her phone buzzing in her pocket.

Throat tight, she fumbled for it.

She saw that it was a text from an unknown number.

The message contained just a single digit.

Five.

23

Kendra knew exactly what the message meant.

It was a prearranged signal for a meet.

Jim Braddock had first suggested the idea when she returned home from Baghdad. And she had argued with him. She wanted to heal, to forget what she had done, but the grizzled old spook had insisted.

Little girl, you never know when hell's going to break loose. Or freeze over. So always, always make sure you've got a backchannel contingency prepped and ready to go. Maybe you're never going to use it. Maybe it's just an extra spoonful of paranoia. But, listen, it's better to have it and not need it than to need it and not have it.

And with that, Jim made her memorise seven locations tied to seven numbers, so if they ever needed to meet under extraordinary circumstances, all they had to do was communicate a number.

Kendra sucked in a breath through her teeth and exhaled sharply.

She never thought that she'd have to use the contingency. But right now, Jim was her only lifeline; her glimmer of hope.

And she needed to get a grip, pull herself together and travel to number five – the library at Saint Lukes Road.

Focus on the objective. Focus.

Kendra rose, feeling light-headed, her knees wobbly. Straightening, she put away her night-vision goggles and glanced at the bodies once more.

It would be all too easy to just leave them lying there like that, but it didn't feel right.

So Kendra backtracked to the dining room. She grabbed the linen covering the grand banquet table and yanked hard, sending cutlery and doilies and candlesticks tumbling.

She bundled up the cloth and returned to the living room. She spread it over the bodies, blanketing them.

Kendra bowed her head. She felt like she should say something dignified, but all she could manage was a hoarse whisper. 'I'm sorry.'

She departed the mansion by retracing her steps through the garage, through the compound, through the back gate. She disengaged the suppressor from her gun and stowed away her ballistic vest.

She re-entered the park and hit the walking track, trying her damnedest to keep her gait casual, normal.

It was still a beautiful day.

The trees were rustling.

Birds were singing.

Kendra stabbed her nails into her palms, internalising her pain.

She tried to reason with herself.

The Hosseinis couldn't have done all of this on their own. Someone has to be supporting them. Instigating them.

The most immediate suspect was VAJA. It was Iran's premier intelligence agency, responsible for conducting black-bag operations and wetwork all around the world.

And yet… Kendra couldn't understand how the Hosseinis could have been recruited.

Leila and Saeed are secular. That's why they were forced to leave Iran after the Islamic Revolution. And that's why they came to New Zealand. To build a new life. A better life. And they've spent years trying to get past the trauma of dislocation and exile. And Ryan? Well, he was born and raised in New Zealand. So why the hell would they get mixed up with VAJA?

Kendra winced.

It didn't make any sense.

None of it did.

And that's when she looked left. She swept her gaze across the pond, and in that instant, she felt her stomach turn, because she realised that she was being followed.

24

The guy was on the walking track on the other side of the pond, moving parallel to her, but he wasn't a jogger.

His posture was all wrong. It was too stiff, too attentive. A virtual giveaway.

But Kendra didn't want to let him know that she had made him. So she kept her face impassive. She just turned away and continued walking at the same pace, as if she had been doing nothing more than admiring the ducks on the water.

Kendra coaxed herself to breathe.

Breathe.

She didn't want to react impulsively.

With the pond separating them, it was clear that the operator wasn't an immediate threat. There was a safety buffer of at least fifty metres. And if he did make a hard and fast move, she was confident that she would see it coming.

That was a small comfort.

Right now, though, Kendra was more concerned about the track directly behind her. It was her blind spot, and she couldn't check it without coming across as being too obvious.

So what do I do?

Skin bristling, fingers flexing, Kendra spotted a bend coming up ahead. And a bicyclist – a civilian – was approaching from the opposite direction. And, yeah, she sensed an opportunity here.

Improvise. Adapt.

Kendra choreographed the moment in her mind.

She knew that she had to execute it perfectly.

As she reached the curve, she smoothly sidestepped to dodge the bicyclist, and the change in angle allowed her to use the edge of her eye to check on her six.

She clocked in another operator.

He was directly behind, maybe less than twenty paces away.

As soon as the bend straightened, he fell out of sight again, and Kendra felt an icy spot forming between her shoulder blades. There was no margin of safety here. He could easily strike at her, and she wouldn't see it coming.

But she swallowed back her anxiety.

She resisted the urge to quicken her steps.

No, they're not going to attack me. Not out in the open. Not with civilians around. If they're going to do it, they'll do it someplace quieter with more foliage.

Kendra rounded another bend in the walking track. This one was sharper, rising to an incline, allowing her more time to scan the shrubbery and treeline to her right, and she didn't see anything that set off her radar.

So... she was only dealing with a tag team of two.

Manageable.

But did these guys belong to the same crew that tailed Ryan at the city centre? Did they have the same intentions?

It was tempting to draw a direct connection, but Kendra didn't think so.

Unlike the other team, this one seemed uncomfortable with the rolling terrain. Their tradecraft was self-conscious, and they were boxing her up way too tight, as if they were more afraid of losing her than concealing themselves.

Kendra took that to mean that they were unfamiliar with Kiwi suburbia, and their training was proving to be a poor fit for local conditions.

They're VAJA operators. Fresh off the plane. Recently deployed.

Kendra wondered what their game plan was. Were they acting as some sort of rearguard for Ryan? Covering for him? Or were they tasked with doing something more?

Kendra thought back to when she opened up the blinds and curtains at the mansion. It seemed harmless at the time. She had only wanted a respite from the darkness, but in hindsight, she may have only revealed herself to watching eyes.

Stupid. Stupid.

Kendra shook her head ever so slightly.

But there was no time to languish in regret now.

What mattered more was that she had no intention of leading these operators to her meeting with Jim Braddock.

That left her with only two options.

She could either ditch them or neutralise them.

25

Kendra decided to neutralise them.

She used her peripheral vision to scan the treeline on her right once more. There was a slope there that led up to a ridge, and so far as she could see, it was clear of civilians.

Perfect.

Kendra inhaled.

One, two, three.

She exhaled.

One, two, three.

She immediately diverted. She stepped off the walking track and on to the narrow path that led up the hill. She felt her leg muscles burn as she climbed, picking up the pace.

Kendra's goal was to split the two operators up.

The one on her tail would no doubt respond by coming after her first. Predictable enough. And the second one would play catch-up. He'd have to circumnavigate the pond in order to reach her.

If Kendra timed this right, the delay would work in her favour.

She would use the first operator as bait to reel in the second.

Yes, she figured that she had a psychological advantage here. VAJA was made up of misogynistic men. They stubbornly believed that a woman's place was in the home because she was capable of little else.

Kendra welcomed that bullshit philosophy.

She relished it because it offered an opening she could exploit.

In her heart of hearts, she knew that she was giving into emotion here, and the smart thing to do would be to disengage from any confrontation. Evade her pursuers and lose them amidst the terrain.

But right here, right now, she was sick of playing it safe, and this was her chance to seize the initiative. She wanted to exact revenge on behalf of the people who'd been murdered in the mansion. And, by God, she was going to make it happen.

When Kendra crested the top of the slope, she stepped off the path. She plunged into the cluster of trees. She chose the widest oak and took cover behind its trunk. Crouching, she unslung her backpack and set it on the grass.

It was a quiet alcove.

Bees were humming from flower to flower.

Shrubs were swaying in the wind.

Kendra waited. Her heart throbbed in her ears, and her body tensed, like a spring wound up to its tightest, ready to explode.

She heard the operator coming up the path.

His footfalls were heavy.

His breaths were laboured.

She peered around the tree. She saw that he had paused. Frustration was etched on his face, and with his hands on his hips, he pivoted this way and that way, and he eventually stepped off the path, trying to see where she had disappeared to.

Kendra clenched her jaw.

She dug her heels into the dirt, and she lunged forward.

The operator turned, his mouth agape, his arms starting to come up in a defensive posture.

Too late.

With her left arm, Kendra swept his defences aside, and with her right arm, she powered through. She caught him in the throat with the webbed skin between her thumb and forefinger. The blow was sharp and precise, and she felt the cartilage in his larynx shatter.

The man jerked forward as if he had just collided against a clothes line, gagging, wheezing, going bug-eyed.

Kendra grabbed him by the lapels of his shirt, cocked her hips to one side and threw him.

He fell into a bush, his arms and legs twitching and contorting inward, his stricken face already turning grey from a lack of oxygen. His mouth was opening and closing like a fish out of water.

Kendra averted her eyes and returned to her hiding place. She picked up her backpack and slung it across her shoulders. Drawing her pistol, she attached the suppressor.

Holding her gun at the low-ready, she waited.

The second operator soon appeared on the path, and the gurgling of his dying comrade lured him in. Stunned, he called out in Farsi and started reaching under his shirt for a weapon.

Kendra wasn't about to let him get that far.

She raised her gun and acquired a sight picture, double-tapping.

The man's head snapped back, and blood dotted the air, and his body went limp. He pitched forward into the bush, straddling his comrade, who convulsed one last time before falling quiet.

Blinking hard, Kendra put her weapon away. She decided against frisking the men. She had caused enough of a ruckus already, and a civilian would stumble upon the scene soon enough.

So she just turned away.

She started brisk-walking in the opposite direction.

26

With her breaths levelling out, she was struck by what she had done. She had improvised an ambush, executed it and snuffed out two lives right in the middle of suburbia.

Shit.

All those hours of therapy – all that psychological reconditioning – had done absolutely nothing to curb her instincts. Because when push came to shove, she had reverted back to her old persona.

The huntress.

Cold. Calculative. Remorseless.

Is that what I am? Is that all that I am?

Kendra performed a surveillance-detection run through the park, twisting, turning, just to be sure that she was no longer being shadowed.

But was she running away from the enemy?

Or was she running away from herself?

Ever since she got back from Baghdad, she'd been caught up in a mental haze, just drifting through life, the days blurring into each other. At one point, she even became a cutter – slicing into her skin with a razor in a desperate attempt to seek relief.

But now... now she felt alive. Yeah, more alive than she'd ever been. Endowed with the singularity of purpose – tracking Ryan down.

Kendra couldn't explain it, but she was consumed by a reckless hunger. A need to reconcile the past and the present. Make things right. And, yes, she would kill anyone who stood in her way.

But at what cost?

Kendra felt the memories of Baghdad blossoming just then, like the stitches of a wound tearing open.

A car bomb detonating like thunder.

Kendra losing her nerve and firing blindly in a dust storm.

A child lying broken and bloodied.

A mother wailing, her eyes accusing Kendra.

The flashback left her mouth shrivelled and dry as dust, and she was suddenly afraid of who she was; of what she was capable of.

But – *no* – she didn't want to think about that right now. She couldn't afford the mindfuck. She had to focus on what was in front of her. Focus on the objective. She had to get to Jim Braddock.

So Kendra exited the park, and eyes darting, emotions raw, she hailed down a passing taxi. 'Can you take me to Mount Albert?'

The taxi driver gave her the once over and nodded. 'Sure thing.'

Kendra got into the back seat.

As they pulled away from Remuera, she checked the traffic behind them. And – *hell* – that's when she realised that she was being followed again.

27

The maroon-coloured Hyundai was two vehicle-lengths back.

Kendra squinted, trying to make out the occupants, but the sun bouncing off the car's windscreen made it too difficult to get a visual.

Frustrated, she tousled her hair.

Was she not aggressive enough with her counter-surveillance in the park?

Goddamn…

Kendra knew she had to deal with this.

She had to fix it.

She turned back to the taxi driver. She sucked in a breath, fidgeted in her seat and broke into a giggle. 'You know what? I've changed my mind. Forget Mount Albert. Take me to Newmarket.'

The taxi driver peered at her through the rear-view mirror. 'You sure?'

'Yep.' She clicked her tongue. 'It's the summer sale today.'

He sighed and rolled his eyes. 'Righto. Newmarket it is.'

'Cheers.'

The taxi driver twisted his steering wheel. He took a turn-off at the next intersection.

Kendra watched the car on her tail peel away from traffic in order to keep up. With the change in angle, the sun's glare was no longer a problem. She could just about make out the silhouettes of three operators – the driver plus two passengers.

Kendra exhaled.

Bingo. I've got you exactly where I want you.

28

Newmarket was the swankiest part of the city. It was filled with upper-crust boutiques, designer cafés and wide boulevards. This was where the fashionable came to dine and shop.

As they cruised down Broadway, Kendra scanned the side streets. It was a metropolitan labyrinth. There were multiple points of ingress and egress, along with plenty of room to manoeuvre, which made for countless diversions.

Kendra checked her six.

The car had closed in.

It was only one vehicle-length behind now.

They want revenge for what I did to their colleagues in the park. That's why they're so eager.

Turning around, Kendra searched for the best place to stop, and she saw it coming up just ahead. It was a bus lane, where a small crowd was embarking and disembarking. Perfect.

'Right there,' she told the taxi driver as she leaned forward and pointed. 'Behind that bus.'

'That's an illegal stop. I can't do that.'

She pouted and tipped her chin. 'Aw, come on. Just this once?'

He hesitated, then shook his head wearily. 'Okay. For you. Just this once.'

'You're sweet.'

As they pulled up to the sidewalk, she pressed a wad of money into taxi driver's hand and stepped out. Plunging into the crowd, she glanced over her shoulder.

As expected, the car on her tail had coasted to a stop as well, and two operators disembarked, fanning out in a pincer movement. They were trying to catch her from both left and right.

Meanwhile, the operator behind the wheel started pulling away from the kerb, revving his car's engine, trying to overtake the bus in his path.

Kendra swallowed.

She knew what he was planning to do.

He wants to get ahead of me and box me in. Give his friends a chance to strike at me from behind.

But Kendra had no intention of making it easy for them.

She needed to disrupt that strategy and force them to reconfigure.

So she zeroed in on the pedestrian crosswalk ahead, and without waiting for the light to turn green, she darted across the street. She zigzagged through the gaps in traffic.

Vehicles honked.

Somebody shouted.

Panting, Kendra reached the sidewalk on the other side.

She rounded the corner.

She was now on a one-way street with traffic flowing from the opposite direction, and the car on her tail couldn't possibly come after her. So the operator had no choice but to bypass the street and orbit around the block.

But the operators pursuing her on foot weren't so easily deterred. They quickly recovered from their surprise and came after her. They were widening their pincer formation now, staring hard, abandoning any pretence at being covert.

With her heart hammering, Kendra picked up the pace to avoid being flanked.

Because there were so many civilians around, she didn't believe that they would use a gun. No, if they really wanted to liquidate her, it would be up close and personal with a needle or a knife.

So don't give them the opportunity. Just don't.

Kendra pivoted into the next street.

She glanced across the road.

For a moment, she considered detouring into the primary school just ahead. She wondered if it would give her more room to manoeuvre; more flexibility to go tactical. But, almost immediately, she dismissed the thought.

Damn it. I can't possibly put children in danger.

Kendra rounded the next corner.

Behind her, the operators were closing in fast, dodging and weaving through the crowd.

Just ahead, the car had reappeared at the intersection, accelerating in.

They're gaining confidence now. They think they have me boxed in.

Kendra craned her neck this way and that way.

She made a snap decision.

Go right.

She veered off the footpath and hurried down the ramp beside her. She entered the parking garage below the Westfield shopping mall.

The smell of exhaust tickled her nostrils, and the sound of squealing tyres filled her ears. She had only one option now – to misdirect her pursuers in the vastness of the mall itself.

29

Kendra ran up the escalator that led into the mall, elbowing and shouldering her way past the shoppers in her path.

When she reached the top, she ventured deep into the complex, taking random turns before ducking into a clothing store.

Kendra picked out a cardigan jacket, a beret cap and lightly tinted sunglasses. She paid for them and put them on immediately. Unslinging her backpack, she hand-carried it loosely by her side.

It wasn't a complete makeover, but at the very least, she had made herself a little less recognisable.

As she stepped out of the store, Kendra spotted one of the operators approaching from her left.

His movements were frantic as he sprinted from shop to shop, and his lips were moving as he spoke into his sleeve. He was obviously in radio contact with his partner, and they had split up in order to search opposite ends of the floor, trying to flush her out.

Kendra inhaled and exhaled.

She walked into the home-improvement store directly opposite and positioned herself at an oblique angle. She pretended to examine a display of porcelain and china.

The operator was closing in now.

She could see him from the edge of her eye.

He was only a few paces away.

She could feel her throat tightening like a screw, and her fingers were flexing.

No sudden moves. Not yet.

The operator lingered and performed a quick scan of the store. With his adrenaline and anxiety clouding his perception, she was counting on him not to recognise her. And he didn't.

Shaking his head, he moved on. His back was now turned, his attention fixed on the next store.

Now.

Kendra stepped out of the store and kicked him on the inside of his knee. She heard it crack, and as he fell, she glided past, snapping her knife open and cutting into his arm. She opened up his brachial artery with a nine o'clock slash.

The operator screamed.

Kendra slipped into the crowd, blending in.

Confused onlookers gasped and murmured. Several people reached down to help him. For all they knew, he was a clumsy young man who had just suffered a fall. A *very* bad fall.

Kendra walked away at a deliberate pace.

Not too fast, not too slow.

She soon spotted the other operator rushing in from the opposite direction. Predictably enough, he had come to the aid of his distressed comrade.

Kendra stretched her lips thin and bowed her head.

The operator passed her by.

Kendra exhaled. She didn't have to worry about him any longer. Because that was the beauty of crippling one pursuer. By doing so, you distracted his partner as well. And with the arterial wound she had inflicted, it was a sure bet that he would have one hell of a time trying to stem the bleeding.

Now all Kendra had to worry about was the operator in the car. She had to assume that he would be parked right in front of the mall, covering the main entrance, trying to catch her if she exited that way. But, no, she wasn't going to use that route. Instead she returned to the escalator and exited the mall via a side entrance.

Eyes darting, she avoided heading back towards Broadway. Instead she threaded her way through several other streets, and once she was sure that she had acquired enough distance, she approached a cab stand.

Kendra selected the last taxi in the row and tapped on the window. 'Gidday. Can you take me to Mount Albert?'

The driver lowered the Kindle he was reading. 'Sure can. Hop on in.'

As they pulled away from Newmarket, Kendra checked her rear.

Nodding in relief, she slipped off her cap and her sunglasses. She was clean.

Finally.

PART THREE

30

Mount Albert was an inner-city suburb that had been built on the remains of an extinct volcano. The streets here curved and rolled. Ethnic shops and restaurants sat on every corner, and the air was tinged with the scent of herbs and spices.

Kendra had the taxi driver drop her off at the intersection of Balmoral and Dominion, and she hit the pavement, performing a surveillance-detection run.

She looped left around the block, then looped right.

She ventured into side lanes that led her past brick-and-tile houses, then doubled back out.

Everything looked good. She had been clean since she got here, and she had stayed clean. And yet… she felt anxious, as if worms were crawling in her veins, chewing her from the inside out.

What was this?

Fear? Doubt? Paranoia?

Blinking hard, she dug out the packet of medication that she carried in her pocket. She popped it open, palmed two pills and slapped them into her mouth. She gulped them, and they went down hard, leaving a bitter aftertaste.

She could only hope that they would keep her going.

But for how long?

It occurred to her that she had pushed herself too hard already; pushed herself too far. And everything that had happened today was putting a terrible strain on her ability to cope.

Maybe she was in real danger of falling off the edge and plunging back into madness.

Kendra shook her head and scrunched up her face.

I have to hold on. I have to see this thing through. For Ryan's sake. For mine.

She performed one last sweep before closing in on the community library. It was a squat building at the bottom of a slope, surrounded by shady trees, charming in a rustic sort of way.

Kendra circled the library, taking the chance to peer through the windows.

She saw only youngsters and pensioners.

Nothing threatening.

She made for the entrance, and the automatic doors whooshed open.

A teenage girl with spiky hair and droopy eyes immediately approached her. 'They say it'll rain the day after tomorrow.'

Kendra hesitated. She sure as hell wasn't expecting this, but the challenge was legit. So she answered with the correct countersign. 'It'd better rain. The grass on my lawn is turning brown already.'

'Here you go.' The girl passed her a sealed envelope, then walked away.

Kendra tilted her head and tore open the envelope.

She unfolded the piece of paper inside.

It was a handwritten note from Jim Braddock.

Meet you at the end of Lyon Avenue.

31

Lyon Avenue was three blocks down.

When Kendra got there, she spotted a black Toyota SUV parked at the end of the cul-de-sac. Its engine was droning, and it flashed its headlights twice. It was a signal that it was safe to approach.

So Kendra did.

As she drew closer, she recognised Jim Braddock in the front passenger seat, looking craggy and grizzled like he always did. He was a bear of a man with the stillness of a Buddha.

She recognised the guy behind the wheel as well. Adam Larsen. He looked sleek and urbane, like he had just stepped off the pages of a Hammett novel.

Kendra popped open the SUV's door and slipped into the back seat, she could feel an undercurrent of nervous energy in the air. It was an unspoken feeling of tension that hung heavy.

She looked at Jim, then at Adam. 'Well, well. Fancy meeting you gentlemen in the neighbourhood.'

Adam thumbed his nose and gave her a thin smile. 'Good to see you too, Kendra. Heard you got held up.'

The concern on Jim's face was fatherly. He reached out and touched her hand. 'The police network's been filled with chatter about disturbances in Remuera and Newmarket. Are you okay?'

'I...' Kendra hesitated and bunched up her shoulders. 'It's been rough and tumble, but I'm managing.'

She gave Jim and Adam a rundown of events. The bombing at the department store. The firefight in the parking garage. What she uncovered at the Hosseini residence. The VAJA operators that she had to neutralise.

When she was done, Jim exchanged a guarded look with Adam. Then he returned his gaze to Kendra. His gravelly voice was soft. 'Little girl, I'm sorry that you had to go through all that.'

Kendra grimaced. 'The hardest thing was what I saw at the mansion. Those people...' She trailed off, then swallowed. 'And VAJA? I just can't bring myself to believe that Ryan could have gotten himself mixed up with terrorism. Or Leila and Saeed, for that matter. It just doesn't... fit.'

Kendra unzipped her bag and reached into it. She dug out a stack of pamphlets. She handed some to Jim and some to Adam.

Adam flicked through. 'It sure looks incriminating.'

Jim tapped his finger. 'Or designed to appear that way.' He shook his head. 'I don't mean to sound indelicate here, but how much do you know about what Ryan's been up to? I mean, since your relationship with him ended.'

Kendra leaned back against her seat and folded her arms. 'To be honest, not a whole lot. When I left ten years ago, Ryan was angry, heartbroken. He yelled at me. Warned me never to contact him. Never to look him up.'

Adam nodded slowly. 'And... that's what you did.'

'Yeah. Yeah, I figured it was for the best. For both our sakes.'

'So you never trawled Facebook or Twitter? Just to sneak a peek at his life every now and then?'

'No, never. Believe me, it was hard. *Fucking* hard.' Kendra tipped her chin. 'But, somehow, I mustered up the self-discipline never to do it. Once or twice, though, I did stumble upon the odd story about the Hosseinis in the New Zealand Herald. Their philanthropy. Their investments. But, even then, I always clicked away. I didn't need the grief.'

'No. No, I'm sure you didn't.' Jim exchanged another look with Adam.

And there it was again – that cagey expression on their faces. That partaking of conspiratorial knowledge, like they were keeping something from her.

The moment stretched into awkward silence, punctuated only by the humming of the SUV's engine.

Kendra thought back to how it all began.

Jim was the father of Section One. It was a black-ops programme that combined civilian intelligence gathering with paramilitary direct action. It allowed small teams of covert operators to find, fix and finish threats anywhere, everywhere.

Adam had been one of those shadow warriors. He was the tip of the spear. Smart enough to gather on-field intel and tough enough to transition into the wetwork.

For all intents and purposes, Section One was a revolution. One that hit fast and hard, neutralising persons of interest, disrupting terror networks. And it laid the groundwork for a new intervention policy – why publicly commit thousands of troops for kinetic action when you can just send in a handful of quiet professionals?

Easy in. Easy out. Seamless.

That is, until an op went bad in Kuala Lumpur, leaving a senior officer named Nathan Raines dead. Then the powers-that-be got cold feet, and they slashed funding. They also muscled through an oversight committee and culled the herd.

Jim was sweet-talked into retiring.

Adam was unceremoniously dumped from Section One.

Kendra, of course, had missed out on all the fun and games. She was already out of the game at the point. Consigned to therapy.

In a sense, they were all in the same boat.

They were star operatives who had been put out to pasture.

Absolutely tragic.

Kendra curled her lip and leaned forward. She jabbed the back of Adam's headrest with her finger. 'Look, I woke up this morning feeling good about myself. Like, shit, I'd actually made some progress. No more moping around. No more feeling depressed. And by lunchtime, I could actually sit in a crowded café and not suffer an automatic panic attack. And that was big for me. *Huge*. Because it felt like I had finally – *finally* – reached a milestone. I was starting to get a grip on all the bad stuff that's been bouncing around in my head. Exorcising all the ghosts. And then...' She shot Jim a disgruntled look. 'Well, Ryan parachuted back into my life, and everything's gone to hell. And – *oh yeah* – innocent people are dead.' She cleaved the air with her hand. 'And, suddenly, I'm dancing with smoke and mirrors, risking my life when I shouldn't have to. And I'm wondering how someone like me goes from a cheerful morning to a shitty afternoon like this. So, for fuck's sake, what aren't you telling me? *What?*'

Adam blinked. He opened his mouth like he was about to respond, but then he hesitated. And he turned to Jim, raising his hands in mock defeat. 'It's your call, Mr Wizard. But, yeah, she deserves to know.'

Jim shifted in his seat and cleared his throat. 'Okay. All right...'

'If you're worrying about my state of mind, well, don't,' Kendra said. 'I've proven myself capable. More than capable. So give it to me straight, minus the sugar-coating.'

Adam smirked. 'She's a tough chick. She can handle it.'

'Fair enough.' Jim nodded, relenting. 'Okay. Let's dial back the clock a little. About six months ago, the GCSB learned that a VAJA operative, code-named Onyx, had arrived in the country. He was posing under the cover identity of Behrouz Farhadi, an Iranian businessman living in exile.'

'What's his real name?' Kendra asked.

'His real name is Karim Movahed. Former colonel in the Quds Force.'

'Bad news, then.'

'Very. Now, through a social dinner, Onyx makes contact with Saeed Hosseini, and from there, he touches base with Ryan. He's looking for software engineers. A pool of talent with a very specific skillset. And Ryan's company seems to fit the bill. This gives the GCSB the jitters, and Trevor Walsh immediately places the Hosseinis under surveillance.'

Kendra shook her head, uneasy.

Trevor Walsh was the director of the GCSB, which was short for the Government Communications Security Bureau. It was an agency that specialised in signals intelligence – the covert interception of data streams.

With bases in Waihopai and Tangimoana, the GCSB's infrastructure acted as a giant sponge, capturing and storing anything transmitted via radio waves, satellite links and hard lines. Algorithms and analysts then trawled through the data, looking for red flags.

What made the GCSB really formidable, though, was that it was also part of Echelon – an intelligence network made up of New Zealand, Australia, the United States, the United Kingdom and Canada. That expanded its scope far beyond the Pacific region, giving it an augmented purview that was almost limitless.

That made a lot of people unhappy, least of all the liberals, which was why legislation had been ushered in to limit the GCSB's influence.

Kendra spoke, 'Walsh doesn't have the authority to spy on citizens without executive approval. That's jurisdictional overreach, and it's illegal.'

Jim shrugged and rubbed his beard. 'Right you are. It is illegal. The GCSB's mandate is very clear – it can only surveil foreign nationals like Onyx. Citizens like the Hosseinis are meant to be off-limits.'

'So why is Walker overstepping?' Kendra asked.

Adam cocked his eyebrow. 'Do you remember Stuxnet? Remember how angry the Iranians were? How they vowed revenge?'

Kendra frowned.

In 2010, Stuxnet was a computer worm that penetrated several Iranian nuclear facilities. It targeted the centrifuges that were used to enrich uranium. As a result, they went haywire, spinning out of control, ripping themselves apart. By some estimates, about twenty percent of the centrifuges were destroyed.

This event was made all the more impressive by the fact that the computers at the facilities were actually air-gapped. That meant that they were operating in insulated networks that weren't connected to the internet. Nonetheless, Stuxnet managed to slip through and infect them anyway, with devastating results.

Officially, no country ever took responsibility for the cyberattack. Speculation was rife in the media, but the West maintained plausible deniability.

However, Kendra knew better.

It was Echelon programmers who had coded the malware, while Israeli agents inside Iran had delivered the actual payload. It was all done in an attempt to prevent Iran from acquiring a nuclear weapon.

In retrospect, though, it didn't stop Iran's efforts at all. It set them back a couple of years, yeah, but it sure as hell didn't weaken their resolve. The Iranians simply hardened their defences and increased their efforts at counter-intelligence.

'So let me get this straight,' Kendra said. 'Onyx is looking for a way to strike back. He wants to do to us what we did to them.'

'Bazinga,' Adam said. 'He wants a Stuxnet-style event, except he's targeting our Echelon infrastructure specifically.'

'Disrupting our eyes and ears?'

'Absolutely. He's going for the crown jewel – Xkeyscore.'

Kendra swallowed, starting to see the endgame now.

XKeyscore was a subdivision within the Echelon system. It was a full-take database that the American NSA ran in cooperation with the GCSB. It allowed agents from both nations to share signals intelligence. It worked pretty much like a search engine, except one that was used for clandestine purposes.

'But we've got the best countermeasures in the world,' Kendra said. 'Coding and distributing malware to cripple XKeyscore is not going to be the easiest thing to achieve.'

'Which is why Onyx zeroed in on Ryan,' Adam said. 'Because his company produces the antivirus software that the GCSB is currently using on its servers at Waihopai and Tangimoana. Who better than him to know what our vulnerabilities are?'

Kendra nodded warily.

Ryan had always been brilliant at computers, and from what she had read in the news, his software had real-time heuristics that were among the best in the industry. It wasn't surprising to hear that his company was responsible for providing cyber security at the GCSB.

If Onyx had compromised Ryan, then all he would have to do was compel Ryan to upload the malware by means of a routine antivirus update. It would bypass all the usual safeguards and act like a Trojan horse, crippling Xkeyscore from the inside out, disrupting covert operations in the Pacific and beyond.

A nightmare.

Adam wagged his finger. 'Ryan's software is designed to repel black-hat penetrations from the outside. But if the source code itself is tainted with a backdoor entry, then you can see how VAJA would be able to take advantage of that.'

'Again, that is why Onyx needs Ryan,' Jim said. 'He has both technical skill and administrative privileges.'

'Exactly.'

Kendra wrinkled her nose. 'Wait. Hold up. I'm sorry, but am I the only one who sees the lapse in logic here? Okay, sure, it's well-known that the Hosseinis are secular Muslims. They hate the *ayatollahs* and the Islamic Republic. So, to get close to them, Onyx poses as someone from a similar background and secures their friendship. I can buy that. But getting Ryan and his company to create a cyberweapon? That's one hell of a red flag. There's no way he would willingly do it.'

Jim shrugged. 'That may be true, but here's something you don't know. Leila and Saeed have been investing heavily in the alternative-energy sector, trying to jump on to the bandwagon. But it appears they've miscalculated. These past few months, their portfolio's gone from bad to worse, and they're desperate to turn that around. Because if they don't, they're facing total financial ruin within a year.'

Adam snapped his fingers. 'The shit's been weighing on Ryan's mind. Clouding his judgement. So, yeah, he doesn't think too hard about accepting Onyx's offer, because the money on the table is too good to pass up. It's cash the family desperately needs.'

Kendra fidgeted, smoothing her hands along her lap. She sighed and shook her head, still reluctant to believe it. 'But this is a cyberweapon we're talking about. Something so obviously malicious and deadly. Ryan wouldn't agree to that. Not in good conscience.'

'Listen, Ryan wasn't required to construct the malware in its entirety. Nope. He only had to build the programmable-logic controller – the artificial-intelligence rootkit. That looked innocent enough because PLCs are used in everything from elevators to assembly lines. So, yes, Ryan could have easily overlooked its true purpose, especially considering the circumstances.'

'So... what? Onyx has different teams in different countries assembling different components?'

'Exactly. And when the time is right, they'll put the entire package together and weaponise it. Prep it for delivery via Ryan's antivirus software.'

Kendra scoffed. 'That's overly ambitious. A ridiculous jigsaw.'

'Which is where the GCSB steps in,' Jim said. 'Walsh puts the Hosseinis between a rock and a hard place. He tells them the truth about Onyx and coerces them to do their patriotic duty – stop a terrorist plot.'

'How?'

'By getting Ryan to go off-spec. Create a PLC that looks legit but in reality isn't. The goal is to sabotage the malware from the moment of conception. Make sure it's dead on arrival.'

'So Walsh turns Ryan into an asset, a mole. But he doesn't have the training for that. He doesn't have the mentality.' Kendra raked her hand through her hair, frustrated. 'Why didn't Walsh just go through Section One? Why take such a big gamble?'

'Because after what happened in Kuala Lumpur, Section One is barely functional, and Deirdre Raines is still dealing with bureaucratic fallout. Our work in counterterrorism? Direct action? It's all under the microscope now. Deirdre couldn't help even if she wanted to.'

Kendra clenched and unclenched her jaw. Her cheeks felt flushed. 'Those operators who were following Ryan in the city centre – let me take a wild swing. They were contractors, weren't they? Hired on short notice?'

'The GCSB's role has always been advisory; to gather and curate intelligence. So, no, they don't have any direct-action capability. That's why Walsh chose to outsource. He got mercenaries to babysit Ryan.'

'Fucking genius. What was in the briefcase Ryan was carrying?'

'The source code and the blueprints for the PLC. He was supposed to pass it to Onyx.'

Kendra thought about the operator that she had been forced to kill in the parking garage. It was a case of crossed signals and mistaken identity. But that didn't make her feel any better about the situation.

Kendra winced. 'Yeah, it all worked out so well, didn't it?'

Adam spread his hands. 'Look, there are two possibilities here. One – Ryan's defected to VAJA. Or two – he's being blackmailed somehow. Either way, he set up those mercs to die.'

Kendra thought about Leila and Saeed. 'It's number two. It has to be. Somehow, Onyx found out he was being played, and he snatches Ryan's parents. And he's using that to strong-arm Ryan.'

'You think?'

'I'm positive. Because if what you're saying is accurate, then Onyx will want Ryan to repair all the holes in the rootkit. Make it fully functional.'

'That's a reasonable enough assumption,' Jim said. 'But here's another complication – Walsh has just placed a kill order on Ryan.'

'He did *what?*'

'Traffic cams showed Ryan fleeing from the scene of the blast. And along with what the police have now found at the mansion, Walsh has gone into full-blown panic. He believes Ryan is the problem, and he now wants to cover his own ass by eliminating him. Because, remember, this whole thing was an unsanctioned op to begin with.'

Adam thumbed his nose. 'Walsh is a moron, and this is exactly what Onyx wants. The GCSB is running around, chasing its own shadow.'

Kendra leaned back against her seat. She exhaled shakily and rubbed her temples. She felt as if her world has just tilted sideways, and everything was unravelling now.

Yeah, a part of her was relieved that Ryan was not a terrorist. It vindicated her faith in him and justified all the tender memories. But another part of her was afraid for him and his family. She wondered if they would even survive this clusterfuck.

Kendra wet her lips, her voice faltering. 'We have to rescind that kill order and get the Hosseinis back. They didn't deserve this. Any of this.'

'Agreed.' Jim nodded. 'It's time we untangled this messy knot.'

'But how? Where do we even begin?'

Adam winked and broke into a grin. 'O ye of little faith. For the record, Jim and I haven't just been sitting around, twiddling our thumbs. We've been doing our homework and following a trail of our own. And, yes, we have a way to find and fix Onyx.'

Kendra straightened, daring herself to hope. 'Tell me.'

32

Piha was only forty minutes away from the city, but the change in the scenery was drastic.

They had left behind the urban sprawl, and they were on the rugged west coast now. The roads here were narrow and twisting, and the landscape was marked by thick rainforest, jagged hills and beaches that featured black volcanic sand.

This was wild and rugged country, and the rural population out here was sparse.

Adam turned off into a side road. Gravel crunched under the SUV's tyres as he manoeuvred through the foliage. Shafts of sunshine filtered through the trees.

Eventually they emerged into a clearing. Just ahead was a wooden cabin that had been built in a quiet alcove, surrounded by palms and ferns. A waterfall cascaded close by, emptying into a lagoon, the water glistening.

It was an idyllic hideaway.

Kendra saw that three Mercedes sedans were parked in front of the cabin. Their plates were diplomatic. Iranian. Meanwhile, eight men with dark jackets and reflective sunglasses were standing around the property. A close-protection team.

Instinctively, Kendra fidgeted and sucked in a breath.

Jim turned in his seat and gave her a reassuring look. 'It's safe, little girl. Trust me.'

'Yeah, I'm trusting you, old man.'

Adam parked the SUV and killed the engine.

They got down, and they were met by one of the bodyguards.

He gestured, his voice flat but polite. 'The ambassador is waiting for you inside.'

'Thank you,' Jim said.

They entered the cabin through the front door, and sure enough, Ambassador Ali Hatami was in the lounge, seated on the sofa. He wore a tailored suit, and he had an Iranian flag pin on his lapel. As was the Persian custom, he wore no tie.

He looked like a Middle Eastern version of Colin Firth, floppy-haired and square-faced, almost too prim and proper for a spartan cabin like this.

He rose and met Jim in an embrace.

They kissed each other's cheeks.

'*Salaam alaikum*,' Jim said.

'*Alaikum salaam,*' Hatami said.

'You look prosperous, my friend. You have put on weight.'

'Ah, just a little. Just a little. The lush Kiwi cuisine is to be blamed.'

'Too many buffets?'

'I'm afraid so. I will have to ease up on them.'

'And how is your wife and children? They are healthy and well?'

'Yes, indeed. My youngest has just started secondary school. She is delighted by the experience. Already she is talking about what she plans to wear to the prom.'

'Mm, they grow up so fast, don't they?'

'Truly.' Hatami sighed. 'We must enjoy our children while we're still able to.'

'I couldn't agree with you more.' Jim nodded. 'Now, you already know Adam Larsen. But may I introduce Kendra Shaw? She is the agent I told you about.'

'*Agha-yeh Hatami.*' Kendra stepped forward, shaking the ambassador's hand. '*Az molaghat-e shomâ khosh vaghtam.*'

'*Khanoom-yeh Shaw.*' Hatami smiled. 'I'm pleased to meet you as well. You speak very good Farsi.'

Kendra demurred, as was the custom. 'That is very kind of you to say. However, I still have a lot to learn. My written Farsi is not as good as I would like it to be.'

'Ah, the willingness to learn is the most important thing. Knowledge follows naturally. This is what I tell my children.' Hatami chuckled. 'Now, would you like some tea?'

Jim nodded. 'Of course. We would love some *chai*. Thank you.'

This was *taarof.* Persian hospitality. The host always offered tea, and the guests never refused.

Hatami spread his hands and gestured. 'Please sit. Allow me to serve you.'

He moved to the kitchen, then returned with an ornate teapot. As they sat on the sofa, he began pouring steaming *chai* into the cups that were already waiting on the coffee table. The rosy smell was fragrant.

Kendra exchanged a glance with Adam, and she saw him pucker his lips and shrug. He was obviously bored by the preamble.

She understood how he felt.

Iranian culture was all about protocol. You had to be gracious. Maintain a dignified appearance. Read in between the lines.

That was hard for Kendra.

Like Adam, she was a scalphunter. Fieldwork was her specialty. Diplomatic sweet-talk? Well, not so much.

More than anything, she wanted to cut through all this bullshit and just get straight to the heart of the matter. However, she kept her simmering emotions in check and willed herself to be patient. She knew that it would be worth it.

After all, Ali Hatami was a rarity in the cutthroat world of geopolitics – a mild-mannered man who had a reputation for being moderate and honourable.

Despite the fraught relationship between Iran and the West, he had managed to negotiate some key breakthroughs. New Zealand food exports were allowed into Iran, while young Iranians could come and study at New Zealand universities.

This set Hatami apart from the ultraconservatives who ran the Islamic Republic. He genuinely wanted bilateral progress. And since Jim had vouched for him, Kendra was willing to give him the benefit of the doubt.

Once Hatami had served them all with tea, he poured a cup for himself and took a seat in the armchair opposite the sofa. Head bowed, he inhaled the fragrance from the tea and took a sip. 'Thank you for agreeing to meet with me. I am in your debt.'

'There is no debt,' Jim said, taking a sip of his tea as well. 'This is what friends do.'

'Please understand, I consider myself a patriot. I love my country. I want what's best for it. This is why I strive to be a good diplomat – I believe peace can be achieved through dialogue and mutual understanding. However, there are days when I feel that this is a hopeless task, because *zahir* and *batin* are in conflict...'

Kendra understood what he meant.

Zahir was the public face that Iranians were expected to show the rest of the world, while *batin* was the private sentiment that was closely guarded and seldom expressed.

Hatami continued, 'Today is one of those days, and I will admit that my faith in my countrymen has been shaken. Please accept my most sincere sorrow for the tragedy in the Auckland city centre. I am deeply ashamed and shocked at what Onyx has done.'

'You had no idea that he was planning this?' Jim asked.

'Ah, I had my suspicions. When Onyx first entered this country under the name Behrouz Farhadi, something about him seemed off. So I performed my own investigation. I learned that his real name was Karim Movahed, and he had a classified military record. Not even my station chief was privy to this fact.'

'He was Quds Force,' Adam said.

'Yes, this is the case. You have to understand, there are many factions within my country. Some are more extreme than others. And Onyx has certainly been drawn into that camp. He became this way when his younger brother in the Revolutionary Guards was killed while protecting a scientist...'

Kendra nodded.

In recent years, several key individuals connected to the nuclear programme had been singled out for assassination. These hits were carried out by Israel's Mossad in an attempt to prevent Iran from acquiring a nuclear weapon. However, just like the Stuxnet cyberattack, these attempts were only partially successful.

Hatami continued, 'I could see that Onyx was running a rogue operation. He no longer cares about national interest. He only thirsts for vengeance. This is why I contacted Trevor Walsh at the GCSB and warned him. I thought that would be enough.'

Kendra clenched her jaw and inhaled. 'Well, apparently not. The situation was mishandled.'

'So it would seem.' Hatami fixed his gaze on Kendra. '*Khanoom-yeh Shaw*, is it true that you have a personal stake in this matter?'

'I do, *Agha-yeh Hatami*. I was there to witness the bombing on Queen Street. And Ryan Hosseini is an old friend of mine. Well, more than an old friend.'

'I see.'

'Will you help us?'

Hatami paused. He took another sip of his tea, then he slowly set the cup down. 'I am not a man of violence. I am a man of reason. As I have said, I have always believed that dialogue and mutual understanding offers the best hope for the future.' Hatami shook his head and sighed. 'But what can one do when faced with unreasoning violence?' Hatami paused again, his eyes narrowing. He cleared his throat. 'Yes, I shall help you. All I ask in return is that once you acquire Onyx, you neutralise him without hesitation. There is no benefit to keeping such a mad dog alive. His actions have proven harmful to the relations between our two nations.'

Kendra leaned forward. 'Rest assured, once I have him in my gunsights, I will put him down. No question about it.'

Hatami gave a small nod. 'Very well. I shall provide you with a contact. The rest will be up to you. *Inshallah*.'

Jim gave a thin smile. '*Inshallah*. Thank you.'

33

Kumeu was an agricultural district marked by creeks and valleys and vineyards. It was evening now, and the sun was beginning to dip, blanketing the rolling countryside with a golden hue. The air smelled of fruity sweetness and pungent manure.

Kendra was lying on the rooftop of a barn.

In her hands, she cradled an Arctic Warfare rifle. It was loaded with ammunition specially chosen for the occasion – glass-capsuled rounds insulated with a sabot and filled with a radioactive isotope.

From her perch, she had good view of the entire farmyard. There were horses on one side, sheep on the other and strawberry fields directly behind.

It was peaceful, secluded.

With the breeze on her face, Kendra leaned into her rifle. She peered through the telescopic sight, scanning far and near.

Jim was positioned to the east.

Adam was positioned to the west.

They were so well concealed within the shrubbery that she couldn't even spot them, which was good.

Between the three of them, she figured they had all the angles of approach covered.

This has to work.

That's when Kendra heard the far-off purring of an engine, and stomach tightening, she swivelled and adjusted her aim. She zoomed in on the long dirt road that led into the farm.

A vehicle was approaching, trailing a plume of dust.

It was a dark-blue van.

Kendra spoke into her throat microphone, 'This is Sierra One. It's game time.'

'Roger.' Jim's voice crackled in her earpiece. 'Let's keep it frosty.'

'Copy that.'

Kendra watched as the van pulled up to the house at the edge of the farmyard. It coasted to a stop, its side door rolling open, and two men leapt out. One of them carried a duffel bag.

They jogged behind the house, disappearing from view.

The van's driver waited and kept the engine idling.

Adam spoke, 'This is Sierra Two. I have a visual. The tangos are inspecting the merchandise. They're being cautious. Running scanner wands all over. Making sure everything's clean.'

'Roger,' Jim said. 'Stand by.'

Kendra waited. Her forefinger lingered just outside her rifle's trigger guard, and her thumb rested on the safety catch. Right now, she was working out all the basic calculations in her head – range, wind speed, barometric pressure. Every possible variable that could throw off her aim.

She wanted to get this right.

She needed to get this right.

Adam spoke, 'Okay. They're satisfied that the hardware is clean. They're finalising the transaction. And... yeah, they're coming back out now.'

'Stand by,' Jim said.

The two men reappeared. The duffel bag was gone, and they were now pushing along two trolleys stacked with boxes. They loaded them into the van and climbed on, sliding the door shut.

Kendra steadied her breaths. She slowed her heartbeat. She flicked off her gun's safety.

The van made a three-point turn and returned to the dirt road, rocking from side to side as it accelerated.

'Sierra One, do you have the solution?' Jim asked.

Kendra planted her cross hairs on just the right spot. 'I have the solution.'

'Scorpio.'

Kendra synchronised her exhale with the squeezing of her trigger, and she felt her rifle buck against her shoulder, and she saw the glass bullet shatter against the van's rear bumper, fragments scintillating in the dying light.

The shot itself was suppressed, and the sound of the impact would have been miniscule, drowned out by the vehicle's engine and the tyres riding on rough terrain. The occupants inside would have been none the wiser.

Kendra immediately pulled back on her rifle's bolt. She sent a spent shell clinking against the rooftop, and she locked the bolt back into place.

She chambered a fresh round. She recalibrated the distance, preparing herself for a second shot in case the first wasn't successful—

But Jim stopped her. 'I'm getting a positive signal. Very strong. You did good.'

Nodding, Kendra relaxed her grip on her rifle.

She watched the van melt into the horizon.

34

The radioactive isotope that had been sprayed against the van acted as a tracer.

It left an invisible trail of breadcrumbs for Adam to follow as he drove, the sensor on his dashboard chirping in a steady tone.

They were leaving Kumeu now, heading back towards the city.

Kendra turned to look at Jim. His seat was reclined, and his eyes were closed. He lay absolutely still. Only his lips were moving, stringing together a Tibetan mantra under his breath. It sounded monotone, throaty.

Kendra turned to look at Adam. He was focused on the task before him. His shoulders were square, and his hands gripped the steering wheel at the ten o'clock and two o'clock positions. His gaze was steely.

The contrast between the two men was sharp.

Serenity versus resolve.

The silence of the moment hung heavy in the space between them, peppered with a blend of anxiety and anticipation.

Sighing, Kendra turned and looked out the window. She stared at the traffic and scenery flying past. All she could do was think about how everything had led to this point.

Ambassador Hatami had tipped them off to the fact that Onyx planned to purchase high-spec computers from a black-marketer named Julius Rowe.

So they had paid Rowe a visit at his hideout in the Henderson Valley. He was a criminal, yeah, but he wasn't without a conscience. When they told him that the computers were going to be used to create a cyberweapon that would harm the country, he immediately did his patriotic duty – he told them about the exchange happening in the farmyard.

Rowe consented to them crashing the party, but he had a caveat – he didn't want it leading back to him. This was why they couldn't install tracking devices on the computers themselves. Because Rowe was nervous about possible blowback.

But Jim had proposed an alternative. By tagging the van with an isotope, they would bypass any counter-surveillance. There was no electronic signature to speak of, and it would allow them to hang back a kilometre or so, avoiding any chance of being spotted.

It was a conceit that was working well so far, like magic. But now Kendra was starting to feel her doubts festering.

Would the van actually lead them to where the Hosseinis were being held? Would the Iranians actually put all their eggs in one basket? What if there was a secondary site?

There was also the added uncertainty of how far Kendra, Jim and Adam could go in this situation. After all, they were performing an unsanctioned op, trying to clean up a mess caused by Trevor Walsh, the GCSB director.

So there would be no support. No backup. No rules of engagement.

Bad. Very bad.

Jaw pinched, face hot, Kendra forced herself to breathe.

In through the nose.

One, two, three.

Out through the mouth.

One, two, three.

She shook her head and reined in her misgivings. Because – *hell* – she needed to make things right and bring the situation full circle. Put an end to all the regrets.

Kendra thought back to 9/11. The global aftershock of the Towers coming down. How it had driven a poisonous wedge between Ryan and her. How it suddenly made it difficult to love a Muslim. All the doubt and hostility and calls for revenge.

Ryan had tried to console her back then. He reassured her that it didn't matter.

But she grew bitter; angry. She felt like she had to choose. And, in the end, she chose the military.

But now? Now Kendra understood that she never should have left. She never should have delivered that foolish ultimatum all those years ago.

And – *oh God* – she remembered that day of days.

...She was standing on the train platform, eyes darting, hands trembling, hoping against hope that he would come, if only to say goodbye, but as the minutes ticked down to zero, grief clawed at her soul, and she couldn't breathe, and when the last boarding call came, she had no choice but to stagger on to the train, and as it pulled away from the station, she pressed her face against the window, her wheezy breaths fogging up the glass, and her eyes were still searching, hoping to catch a glimpse, hoping to find respite, but there was nothing, no hope, and she broke down in a haze of tears, realising that he hadn't come...

Jim's voice dashed her memory. 'You still with us, little girl?'

nked hard and looked at Jim. His eyes were still
now wore a grave expression on his face.

, old man.'

iving out bad energy. I can feel it.'

'Just...' Kendra swallowed. 'Just remembering.'

'Have you ever heard of the concept of *samsara*?'

'No. Can't say I have.'

'It's the cycle of *karma*. Cause and effect. We're destined to
keep making mistake after mistake until we reach spiritual
maturity. Only then are we able to start redeeming ourselves. And
it all starts with acceptance. Letting go. Because, hey, beating
yourself up over what could have – *what should have been* – is
absolutely the wrong way to look at your journey. In fact,
everything that's happened has led you here. Geared you up for
this moment. And that's why you find yourself at the precipice of
change.'

Kendra nodded slowly. 'I think I get what you're trying to
say.'

'Do you?'

'We have to keep fucking up until we learn how to do what's
right.'

'In a nutshell. Now, listen, when we get there, regardless of
what we find ourselves up against, I want you to take point on
this op.'

Kendra frowned. 'Me? You want me to take charge?'

Jim nodded. 'This is personal for you. Ryan is personal. And
after all that's happened today, you deserve to be the tip of the
spear.' He opened his eyes and tilted his head towards Adam. 'Do
you concur, Wonder Boy?'

'Oh, I do concur.' Adam thumbed his nose and grinned.
'And, yeah, I forecast that the odds are strongly tipped in our

favour. A New Age geezer, a washout and a mental patient. VAJA will never know what hit them.'

Despite herself, Kendra smiled. 'Thank you. Thank you both for being here for me.'

'That's what friends are for. Remember – ours is not to question why. Ours is to do or die.'

35

About ten klicks out from Kumeu, the van's trail suddenly deviated from the North-Western Motorway. It swung towards Massey, then looped around the Henderson Valley, then angled back towards New Lynn before rejoining the motorway once more.

It was a meandering route; circuitous.

But Kendra knew the VAJA operators weren't just enjoying a sightseeing tour. They were executing a surveillance-detection run. They were alternating between a densely populated area and a lightly populated one, using the difference in rhythm to flush out any shadows.

Kendra wondered how much of it had to do with the way she had hurt them this afternoon. She wondered if it had forced them to be more self-aware, more cautious.

But, ultimately, it didn't really matter. The radioactive isotope would allow Adam to hang back and patiently track them from a distance.

At Western Springs, just shy of the city centre, the van deviated once more. It entered Grey Lynn and crisscrossed side streets, then orbited back out.

There seemed to be an increase in urgency here; an uptick in tempo.

The van now raced towards Sandringham, then Epsom, then it descended the Greenlane off-ramp and entered the Southern Motorway.

Kendra felt her anticipation rising, like fire in her blood.

She could see the pattern now.

Ever since the van left Kumeu, it had been consistently moving in a single direction. Sure, there were diversions, but they were always momentary. And the van always swung back towards the south, towards Manukau, as if that was the centre of gravity, the intended destination.

Why would they be taking so many damn countermeasures unless the endpoint is their base of operations? This has to be it.

The van continued on for two klicks, then it detoured by mounting the Ellerslie-Panmure on-ramp. It circumnavigated the roundabout, then it rejoined the motorway once more.

Another five klicks.

The van branched off into Sylvia Park, and after a quick loop, it returned to the motorway once again.

Kendra shifted in her seat, chewing on her lip.

She was certain now.

This is it.

The van travelled for another seven klicks, then it pulled off the motorway for the final time.

It entered Highbrook Drive, and an industrial park loomed. A swathe of factories and warehouses were nestled amidst landscaped fields and gleaming waterways.

This was where the signal ended.

Kendra straightened, her eyes big. 'We're here, aren't we?'

Adam inhaled and nodded. 'We're here.'

36

Twilight had given way to darkness.

Kendra, Jim and Adam were crouched behind a line of trees, studying the warehouse that lay in the gully below. There was no perimeter fence. Just a ring of grassland that stretched out for a hundred metres in every direction.

Directly behind the warehouse lay the waters of Curlew Bay, its waves lapping gently in the breeze, and the humming of insects was interspersed with the droning from the motorway in the distance.

With her monocular pressed against her eye, Kendra scanned the terrain over and over. She memorised the sight lines and calculated all the angles of approach. And she could feel that electric buzz in her muscles. That combination of anxiety and exhilaration.

This has to be ground zero.

Lowering her monocular, Kendra sucked in a breath. 'There are only three tangos patrolling the grounds. That's very light security for such a big area. But I have a feeling that's done on purpose.'

'Mm-hm.' Adam scanned the place through a pair of binoculars, smirking. 'It's way more subtle than you would usually expect from VAJA.'

Jim peered through the scope of his Arctic Warfare rifle. 'It's a practical choice. They don't want anything showy or overt. And by leasing a warehouse in an industrial district, they get to move personnel and equipment in and out without drawing any attention.'

'Yep. And the fact that they're deviating from their usual modus operandi means that something different is happening here. Something big.'

'So how did they manage to keep this place off the GCSB's radar?' Kendra asked.

Jim tilted his head. 'My guess is that the warehouse is completely off the grid. No active internet connection. No uncontrolled phone calls. No stray signals. But, at the same time, they're careful to maintain the guise of legitimacy. They've registered it as a packaging company, complete with a functional skeleton staff. But for the real meat and potatoes? They rely on old-fashioned tradecraft.'

'Meaning couriers.'

'Correct. Whenever something needs to be coordinated, they do it through passive communication. And whenever they need to secure something – software or hardware – they just send the couriers out to get them.'

'Makes sense,' Adam said. 'It would be painstakingly slow, especially in this age of instant gratification, but it's the best way to maintain operational security.'

Kendra considered that for a moment, and she thought back to the VAJA operators she had encountered in Remuera and Newmarket. She recalled the way they had behaved – the lack of agility, the reckless improvisation. It made sense now.

Kendra nodded. 'If they have to resort to wireless communication, it's going to be limited to a small radius. And from what I've seen, I think they're using two-way radios. FRS models with a range of under ten klicks.'

Jim turned away from his rifle's scope and looked at Kendra. 'That sounds about right. Which means their command-and-control structure is going to be isolated. Onyx is pretty much running the show on his own with minimal input from his handlers.'

Adam lowered his binoculars and wobbled his head. 'Well, whoopee. We won't have to worry about a quick-reaction force coming down on our asses when we make the breach.'

'So this is it,' Kendra said. 'All their eggs in one basket.'

'It has to be. It wouldn't make sense to have multiple black sites. Not with such limited communication. That's why they fucked up their attempts on you in Remuera and Newmarket to begin with – it's impossible for Onyx to issue orders to operators in the field. So, yeah, right now, he's going to play his cards close to the vest.'

'Locking down the Hosseinis and the PLC component in one location.'

'Yeah. It makes all the variables easier to control,' Adam said. 'Remember – he's already taken enough risks today. He has every reason to be conservative.'

'I concur.' Jim reached into his bag. He pulled out a tablet computer, and with a flick of his finger, he powered it on.

But unlike regular tablets, this one had a screen that used red light instead of white. It restricted the glare and kept it localised, and no one beyond their immediate vicinity would be able to spot it.

Jim launched an app and keyed in the address for the warehouse, and immediately, a wireframe model blossomed. A complete layout of the structure.

Kendra leaned in, her eyes squinting.

'Courtesy of the Israelis,' Jim said. 'They're constantly dealing with terror strikes within their borders. So they always have a complete collection of schematics for every building in their country. And, yes, the GCSB thought it might be a good idea to quietly do the same here.'

'Big Brother personified.' Adam whistled softly. 'Usually, I'd be throwing a hissy fit and calling this an intrusion of civil rights. But, right now, hey, I'm just happy to have it.'

Jim swiped his finger and zoomed in on the virtual model. He panned this way and that way. 'So... we're looking at two levels here. The main floor of the warehouse itself, and catwalks and balconies on the second floor, with offices all around.'

'It's a damn shooting gallery,' Kendra said, her nostrils flaring. 'Look at all the overlapping fields of fire. Whether you're up or down, you're constantly exposed.'

'Right you are, little girl. Which is why we won't be going in loud.' Jim reached into his bag and pulled out a strange-looking grenade. He tossed it to Kendra. It was all sharp angles and polished chrome. 'We'll stealth it like ninjas and rearrange the pieces on the board to our advantage.'

Adam grinned. 'Copy that, Mr Gandalf.'

37

Kendra and Adam circled around and approached the warehouse from the rear.

It offered the path of least resistance. The sentries were mostly patrolling the front of the building or the sides. They weren't really expecting anyone to intrude from the water's edge, hence their rounds of the area were less frequent.

Kendra intended to exploit that.

She moved in a slow, careful shuffle, leaning into her UMP sub-machine gun, night-vision goggles clasped against her eyes.

Everything felt heightened now.

The grass brushing against her shoes.

The wind caressing her face.

Her laser dancing over the eerie green glow of the terrain.

There was almost no moonlight, thanks to the presence of a heavy cloud cover, and that reassured Kendra. So long as she didn't stray too close to the lamp posts or spotlights dotting the warehouse's perimeter, she would remain invisible to the naked eye.

Still, she wasn't relying on shadows alone to achieve cover and concealment.

She had selected a route that took her through the most rugged parts of the terrain. Places where the topography rose or fell, further obscuring her silhouette.

Eventually Kendra stopped and went prone, flattening herself against a grassy knoll.

Beside her, Adam did the same. He set down his submachine gun and unslung the HK69 grenade launcher he'd been carrying. He braced it against his shoulder.

The paved parking lot was twenty metres ahead, and just beyond that was the loading dock. This was as close as they could get without coming into range of the CCTV cameras.

'This is Sierra Actual. We're in position,' Kendra said into her throat microphone. 'We're good to go.'

'Copy, I'm providing overwatch,' Jim said. 'Ready whenever you are.'

'Wilco. Stand by.' Kendra turned to Adam and nodded.

'Executing now.' Adam aimed his launcher skyward and squeezed the trigger.

The launcher thumped, and the grenade soared in an arc, spiralling as it did.

It disappeared somewhere beyond the warehouse's rooftop.

A moment later, all the lights in and around the warehouse went dark.

The grenade had detonated without a sound, unleashing an electromagnetic pulse that fried all the circuitry within range, disabling not only the power supply but any communications equipment.

Kendra rose to her feet. 'Moving.'

'Covering.' Jim said.

Kendra and Adam entered the parking lot. There were three cars here. Sedans. She recognised the one in middle as being the vehicle that had pursued her this afternoon.

Working quickly, she got her knife out and slashed their tyres. She didn't want them going anywhere in a hurry. Then she was up and moving again, trotting towards the loading dock.

'Hold up,' Jim said. 'Tango approaching at your two o'clock.'

With her breath caught in her throat, Kendra raised her fist and signalled Adam to drop to a crouch. Then she pivoted and aimed her weapon in that direction.

Sure enough, a sentry rounded the corner, a couple of paces away. He was smacking his palm against his radio, muttering in frustration.

'I have the solution,' Jim said.

'Scorpio,' Kendra whispered.

There was a pop, followed by a spray of blood and brain matter, and the sentry staggered and sprawled forward against the ground.

'Tango neutralised,' Jim said. 'You're clear to proceed.'

38

Kendra sidled up by the side door that led into the loading dock's interior. She covered Adam as he inspected it for tripwires before picking the lock.

She counted down the seconds in her head. She felt her anxiety rise, and she really wished they could move faster.

But, no, they couldn't just blast their way in.

By now, Onyx would be gauging the blackout as suspicious, especially since he had lost radio contact with his sentries on the perimeter. But he wouldn't resort to executing the Hosseinis. Not until he was sure that an all-out assault was taking place.

So, for their sake, Kendra needed to preserve that element of ambiguity. Maintain the silence for as long as possible.

'Open sesame.' Adam unlocked the door and pushed it inward, hinges squeaking.

Kendra nodded, sweeping her weapon back and forth. 'Making entry.'

They cleared the doorway and the common area beyond, then pushed forward into a maze of crates and containers and forklifts. The air smelled of polystyrene and plastic, and with the air conditioning disabled, the temperature was rising.

Kendra could feel sweat beading on her forehead and pooling under her armpits. She sliced the corners, eliminating the blind spots, and soon enough, she spotted a van parked on the far side of the loading dock.

It was the same one that had visited the farmhouse earlier.

With Adam covering her, Kendra slashed the van's tyres.

That's when Jim's voice crackled in her earpiece. 'Sierra Actual, listen up. The two other tangos on the perimeter are getting antsy. One looks like he's going to enter the building through the front entrance.'

Kendra curled her lip.

Was the sentry heading inside just to grumble to Onyx? Or to warn him that something was afoot?

Ultimately it didn't matter. She didn't want the stress level getting any higher than it already was. So the choice was clear.

'Knock them both down,' Kendra said.

'Ten-four.' There was a pause, followed by the suppressed thump of the sniper rifle cycling twice, then the sound of Jim exhaling. 'Tangos neutralised.'

'Stay frosty.'

Kendra and Adam ascended a ramp and slipped into the corridor that led into the warehouse's main floor.

39

There were voices echoing from just ahead.

Men were shouting back and forth in Farsi.

Kendra reached an intersection in the corridor and crouched beside the corner. She strained to listen.

'What are they saying?' Adam whispered.

Kendra tilted her head. 'Onyx is yelling for someone to turn on the backup generator. And another guy is yelling back. Saying he doesn't know where it is. And Onyx is frustrated. He's worried about corrupted data because all the computers have gone dead—'

Suddenly a light glowed from the corridor ahead, and Kendra's heart skipped.

She eased back behind the corner.

Footsteps were approaching. A VAJA operator was carrying a flashlight. It was almost certainly an old-fashioned model. One that ran on an incandescent bulb, which why it was still functioning despite the electromagnetic pulse.

The footsteps got louder and closer.

Kendra gritted her teeth.

The operator marched right past the intersection. He didn't notice Kendra and Adam huddled against the wall, just below his eyeline.

Adam tracked the guy with his laser.

Kendra reached out and gave Adam's shoulder a squeeze.

Adam hit him with a three-round burst.

The operator's body seized up in mid-stride, and he fell. His flashlight clattered against the floor, rolling.

Kendra duck-walked towards it. She picked it up and switched it off.

40

For Kendra, functioning flashlights were a problem.

It meant that Onyx and his men weren't totally blind. Sure, their field of vision was limited, and their situational awareness was impaired, but if push came to shove, they could still organise themselves and put up a fight.

Not ideal.

But Kendra reassured herself that the presence of flashlights could also work in her favour. Assuming each operator carried one, the illumination would act as beacons in the dark, making it easier for her to pinpoint their positions and react accordingly.

Also, the current situation was much better than the alternative – being forced to go up against operators equipped with night-vision. That wasn't the case here. Even if they had that kind of gear, the electromagnetic pulse would have fried their circuits by now, rendering them useless.

Kendra wiped sweat off her brow and exhaled.

We still have the advantage here.

She watched Adam as he patted down the dead operator.

He looked up. 'No body armour. Armed only with a Beretta 9mm.'

Kendra nodded, her confidence buoyed. 'Good. Let's hope it's the same for the rest of them.'

'Roger that.'

They continued moving. They crept to the end of the corridor and button-hooked into the hallway beyond. They entered the warehouse's main floor.

They were faced with rows of pallet racks that soared, creating narrow aisles that evoked a feeling of claustrophobia.

Even more daunting was the presence of cantilevered balconies and intersecting catwalks hanging from above. It allowed operators on the second floor to simply peer over and observe the ground floor below.

Tactically, it was a nightmare. Overlapping fields of fire. Sight lines that were less than clean. And choke points everywhere.

Kendra grimaced. It was one thing to see the warehouse represented as a wireframe model, and it was another thing altogether to be actually here, experiencing it for real.

It's a damn shooting gallery. Danger from up high. And danger from down below.

The only option now was to advance in a leapfrog fashion. Navigate the aisles slowly and cautiously.

So Kendra held her position and covered Adam while he inched forward a couple of paces. Then Adam held his position and covered her while she inched forward a couple of paces.

Over and over, they repeated the drill.

The seconds seemed to stretch into forever.

Eventually Kendra spotted signs of illumination coming from up ahead, where the voices echoed. So that's what she zeroed in on.

Tension knotted up her stomach, and her fingers flexed around her weapon. She sidled up beside a rack. She peered through a gap between the two cartons sitting on the shelf in front of her. And – *fuck* – that's when she saw Ryan.

41

That moment of moments was like a million pinpricks on her soul. Searing. Red-hot. And she felt everything at once.

Longing.

Anger.

Regret.

There he was, seated in a chair in the clearing ahead, facing a row of modular desks kitted out with widescreen monitors and towering workstations. Wiring and power boards lay at his feet, snaking all around.

On the far right were his parents, Leila and Saeed, seated in two chairs pushed against a wall. They were bound and gagged, looking terrified but otherwise unharmed.

Ryan, though, wasn't so lucky. His face was puffy and bruised, and his posture was despondent.

Hovering close by was Onyx, flanked by two operators carrying flashlights. He was pacing back and forth, smoking a cigarette, its tip burning in the darkness. His movements were sharp and agitated, like he was on the verge of losing control.

Kendra lifted her gaze. There was another operator positioned on the catwalk directly above. That realisation caused her throat to cramp up.

If they launched an assault on Onyx now and tried to free Ryan, it meant that the operators could very well respond by turning their guns on Leila and Saeed. But the reverse was also true. If they tried to free Leila and Saeed first, Onyx could decide that there was nothing left to lose and proceed to murder Ryan.

Kendra shook her head. She settled on the only option left – a simultaneous assault executed with split-second timing. There would be no room for error.

Turning, Kendra looked at Adam and gestured. 'You need to get up there. Take out the operator above.'

Adam nodded and gave her arm a reassuring squeeze. 'I will be waiting on your mark. And don't worry. I'll get it done.'

'I know you will.'

Adam shuffled back down the aisle and disappeared around the corner. He headed for one of the stairwells that led up to the second floor.

Kendra inhaled deeply, then spoke into her throat microphone. 'Sierra One, we have eyes on the principal and the precious cargo. And we're going to go loud. I need you covering the front entrance. Cold zero.'

'Roger,' Jim said. 'Cold zero.'

With her eyes fixed on Onyx, Kendra unclipped a stun grenade from her combat chest rig and readied it in her hand.

42

'This is Sierra One. In position,' Jim said. 'Covering the entrance. Cold zero.'

Kendra waited for Adam, the edges of her mouth crinkling. She could imagine him creeping up the staircase now. He would be hugging the shadows, positioning himself to take out the operator on the catwalk.

Finally she heard his voice. 'This is Sierra Two. In position. Good to go.'

Kendra could see his laser puncturing the darkness, hovering on the unsuspecting operator.

She swallowed. Everything had led up to this hair-trigger moment, and what it would come down to now was speed, surprise and violence of action.

Gritting her teeth, Kendra pulled the pin on her stun grenade. 'Bang and clear. Three, two, one. Execute.'

43

Kendra hurled the stun grenade out into the clearing, and it detonated.

The concussive blast was like thunder and lightning combined, and Onyx and his operators flinched, confused.

That's when Adam opened fire, hitting the operator on the catwalk.

He convulsed from the bullet impacts, his torso twisting, and he dropped off the platform, plunging straight down, landing with a god-awful crunch on the ground floor.

Kendra swung out of cover, adrenaline scorching her senses. She fanned her trigger, hitting the operator closest to her with a three-round burst, followed by another. He fell against a desk, overturning a workstation.

Kendra swung her aim around and tracked the remaining operator. But he already had his weapon raised – a Skorpion machine pistol. She didn't give him the chance to use it. She hit him with a three-round burst, then another, and he went down.

Kendra pivoted, trying to bring her gun to bear on Onyx—

But she froze when she saw Onyx grabbing Ryan, yanking him from his chair, using him as a shield. Onyx had his left arm locked across Ryan's neck, his left hand holding a flashlight. In his right hand, he had his Skorpion raised over Ryan's shoulder.

Shoulders tight, Kendra tried to line up a shot, but her hands were shaking, and she couldn't do it.

Damn it.

That's when Onyx aimed the flashlight in her eyes, and she felt her night-vision goggles dim.

Going on instinct, Kendra ducked and rolled as Onyx opened up on her, his gun's muzzle flashing like a strobe, bullets ripping into the shelf in front of her.

A chorus of sparks screamed.

Shredded packaging misted the air.

The stench of gunsmoke was overpowering.

Panting, ears ringing, Kendra picked herself up and darted down the aisle. She swapped her half-spent magazine for a fresh one. Then she reached the other end of the rack, slicing the corner, repositioning herself to outflank Onyx, hoping to get a better angle.

But when she came around, she saw that Onyx and Ryan were gone.

44

Frantic, Kendra jerked her aim this way and that way.

Adam's voice crackled in her earpiece. 'Onyx is making a break for the entrance.'

Kendra grimaced and glanced at Leila and Saeed. They had fallen off their chairs and were now huddling in the corner, still bound and gagged. They looked frightened but unharmed.

Kendra nodded. 'Roger, Sierra Two. Lock down this location, and keep the precious cargo safe. I'm going after the principal now.'

'Stay frosty.'

Kendra quick-stepped past the computers in the clearing.

She entered the reception area.

Onyx was dragging Ryan backwards. They were almost to the door.

Onyx pressed his gun against Ryan's temple. He yelled in English, 'Get back. *Get back.*'

Kendra spoke in Farsi, '*Agha-yeh Movahed*, it's over. Let him go.'

Onyx frowned at the mention of his real name. 'Over? No, it's not over.' He tightened his grip, choking Ryan and causing him to whimper. 'Allow me to walk out of here and I will release him. Otherwise I will kill him.'

Kendra stared into Ryan's eyes. 'You don't want to do that. That would be a mistake.'

'I *will* kill him.'

Kendra inhaled. She steadied her aim and acquired a sight picture. She flicked her weapon's selector switch to semi-auto. But Onyx was careful to keep his body directly behind Ryan, blocking any possible shot.

Damn it.

Kendra exhaled, her mouth dry, her chest stitched tight.

That's when she heard Jim's gravelly voice. 'This is Sierra One. I have the solution.'

'Scorpio,' Kendra whispered.

Onyx smirked. 'What did you say?'

The glass door behind Onyx cracked, and it sounded as if an angry hornet had buzzed into the room.

Onyx's hand – the one holding the gun – exploded, splattering Ryan's face with blood. Severed fingers pinwheeled through the air. The gun dropped, and Onyx screamed, loosening his grip on Ryan.

Ryan managed to swing his elbow back into Onyx's stomach and squirm out of his grasp.

Now.

Kendra advanced as she shot Onyx. Twice in the chest. Once in the forehead.

Onyx stiffened and staggered, thudding against the glass door before sliding down to the floor, leaving a trail of crimson behind him, his face contorted in a final death stare.

Breathing through her teeth, Kendra yanked off her night-vision goggles. Then she reached out and enveloped Ryan in the fiercest hug, never wanting to let go.

'Kendra? Is that you?' Ryan stammered, shivering.
'Yeah, baby. It's me.'

PART FOUR

45

It was a pristine morning.

Clear skies.

A gentle breeze.

Kendra held Ryan's hand as they approached the burnt-out husk of the Farmers department store. The entire intersection had been cordoned off with yellow tape and warning signs.

There was a feeling of desolation here; melancholy.

It was the one spot in the entire city centre that traffic no longer visited.

Ryan laid a wreath of fresh flowers at the sidewalk memorial, placing it amidst the overflowing mounds of gifts and cards and pictures. Then he stepped back and studied all the items on display for a moment. He bowed his head. His eyes fluttered.

Kendra squeezed his hand. 'What are you thinking, baby?'

'I'm thinking...' Ryan hesitated, and he sighed. 'Well, I don't know what to think. I feel sad. And responsible. And confused.'

Kendra gave a small nod, understanding that words couldn't possibly do justice to all the pent-up emotions. 'It's survivor's guilt. I know. I've been there.'

'Does it ever get better?'

'Yes. If you take things day by day.'

Ryan gave Kendra an uncertain smile, and he wrapped his arm around her shoulder. He drew her close and breathed in her hair. 'My parents are inviting you for dinner. They want to say thank you. And they want to start over.'

'Mm. A second chance?'

'Yeah. A second chance. Seems like we shouldn't take that for granted.'

Kendra knew exactly what Ryan meant.

As a show of gratitude for stopping Onyx, the prime minister herself had personally intervened in their case. She had classified all evidence that the Farmers blast was an act of terror and adjusted the facts so that it looked like the Hosseinis had been kidnapped for ransom, only to be rescued at the eleventh hour.

Ambassador Ali Hatami, for his part, had smoothed things over between both governments by organising a clandestine relief fund. It would take care of the survivors of the bombing, as well as compensate those who had lost loved ones.

However, any admission of guilt was off the cards. All backchannel inquiries with the ultraconservatives in Tehran were met with the staunchest of denials. No, Onyx wasn't part of VAJA. He was a common criminal, exiled from Iran long ago because of un-Islamic activities. And, naturally enough, they refused to accept any responsibility for his actions. And maybe it was just as well that they didn't. Maybe it was cleaner that way.

For Kendra and Ryan, the first couple of days after were tough. There were a lot of tears, a lot of explanations, and they struggled to reconcile all the contradictions.

At times, the anguish almost seemed to be too much.

But – *thank God* – they had come out of that storm okay.

They were settling down now, finding their rhythm, healing.

No, it wasn't perfect, but it was as good a start as any.

Kendra looked up at Ryan and gazed into his eyes. 'I'm glad I found you again. And as ugly as all of this is, we'll find the light at the end of the tunnel. We will.'

'Do you really believe that?'

'I have to.'

Ryan gave her an earnest smile this time, and cupping her face, he pressed his lips to hers, tender at first, then passionate.

The kiss went on and on.

And Kendra never wanted it to end.

46

Kendra met the Hosseinis for dinner at the Pacifica Hotel.

This was unusual, to say the least. *Taarof* – Persian hospitality – usually demanded that the hosts invite a guest into their home and cook a meal for them.

However, after recent events, Kendra could understand why the Hosseinis couldn't return home to Remuera. It was now a place of haunted memories. Where innocent blood had been shed.

The trauma was still fresh.

So staying at a hotel was the best option.

For her part, Kendra was nervous about meeting Leila and Saeed again. She wasn't sure what they would think of her, especially considering the acrimonious history they'd shared. So she had fussed over her hair and make-up. She wanted to look soft and demure. She figured the Hosseinis liked soft and demure.

In the end, though, Kendra didn't have to worry about surface appearances at all.

Leila and Saeed seemed genuinely excited to meet her, and they were quick to embrace her and kiss her cheeks. They were warm and obliging, and as they sat down for dinner and the wine and conversation flowed, all Kendra's doubts and fears melted away.

It was obvious that the Hosseinis had changed. They were now more mellow, less judgemental. Eager to give her the acceptance and respect that she had craved for so long.

At one point, Leila even reached across the table and held Kendra's hand. '*Astaghfirullah*. We misjudged you. We should not have. We are in your debt.'

Kendra could only smile. 'There is no debt. This is what friends do.'

Saeed gave a hearty chuckle and tapped the table. 'Only the best of friends.'

Ryan raised his wine glass. 'Well, then. To friendship.'

Kendra raised her glass as well. 'To new beginnings.'

And with that, they clinked their glasses together, turning a new page in their relationship. The past didn't matter anymore. Only a better future.

47

'Well, Kendra, you certainly seem happier than the last time I saw you. Can you tell me what's changed?'

Kendra was seated on the sofa in her therapist's office. Dr Ropata was studying her through half-moon glasses, a measured smile on his lips.

Kendra sighed. 'Well, a lot's changed. I've reconnected with old friends. And I've come to realise that there's more to life than just putting myself in a box and agonising over the past.'

'You want to break out of that box?'

'I want to expand my horizons, yeah.'

'Good on you for making such a conscious effort.'

'Well, I have hurt, and I have been hurt. But I make my own choices. I see no reason to hide it. I am who I am. What's important from here on out is the future.'

'That's right. Mark Twain once said that we should plan for the future because that's where we're going to spend the rest of our lives.'

'Makes sense.' Kendra chuckled and nodded. 'Right now, though, I'm happy. Hell, I'm happier than I've been in ten years. And that's more than enough.'

NOTE FROM THE AUTHOR

Hello there. John Ling here. I hope you've enjoyed reading my story as much as I've enjoyed writing it.

Do you have questions? Comments? Critiques? I'd love to hear from you. Please get in touch with me by visiting my website at johnling.net.

You can also sign up for my mailing list. You'll be kept up to date on exclusive events and giveaways. Yes, I have lots of cool stuff to give away. Don't miss out.

I look forward to hearing from you!

Cheers.

EXCERPT: THE BLASPHEMER

Abraham Khan is a Muslim who dreams of changing the world. He's liberal, pro-Western and determined to speak out against the extremists who have hijacked his religion. That makes him a target, and the consequences hit him fast and hard – an armed fanatic smashes into his home one evening, trying to kill him. He survives the harrowing attempt, just barely, but will he survive the next one?

Maya Raines is the special operator brought in to protect Abraham. She is tough and committed. The very best at what she does. Always one step ahead of the threat.

But Abraham is no ordinary principal – he will not hide, and he will not stay silent. And as rage explodes on the streets and the nation is propelled to the brink, Maya will have to ask herself the hardest question of all: *how far would you go to protect one man's right to speak?*

When you want to know how things really work,
study them when they're coming apart.

William Gibson, Zero History

PART ONE

1

Samir had decided that tonight would be the night.

As he sat in his car with the engine off, he stared at the house across the street. The rain had eased to a trickle, and he could see movement past the windows. The man of the house was helping his wife set the table for dinner. Curtains billowed, hiding the man's face. But Samir knew it had to be him.

The apostate.

The blasphemer.

Samir exhaled, feeling so many things at once. Joy and hate. Faith and doubt. Excitement and fear. Which was which? He could no longer tell. Pain started to bloom in his temples, and he could feel it reaching into his eyeballs, stabbing him in sync with his heartbeat. That damn headache was back.

He clenched his jaw, trying to tough it out. He didn't want to medicate himself. Didn't want to risk dulling his senses, blunting his edge. But in the end, the migraine proved too crushing, too searing, and he relented. A bit of pain was good for the spirit, yes, but too much would be a hindrance.

Opening his glove box, he pulled out a paracetamol blister pack. The foil packaging crackled and popped as he pressed out two pills. He had no water, so he dry-swallowed them. It took him three tries and a fair bit of retching before they went down.

Breathing through his teeth, he was tempted to lean back against his seat. To close his eyes. To wait for the pain to fade. But he stopped himself. For a week now, he had barely slept and had eaten only a little. The fasting had purified his soul but wrecked his body. Nodding off now would be too easy. Far too easy. So he forced himself to stretch, to straighten.

Yes, tonight would be the night. God had chosen him to be a *mujahid*. A holy warrior. He knew he had to obey.

Unzipping the bag beside him, he pulled out a pistol. It gleamed black, looking like the ugliest thing, its icy metal chilling him through his glove. Biting his lip, flexing his fingers, he raised the gun, uncomfortable with how big and heavy it felt. It was a Norinco. A .44 calibre. The Asian guy who had sold it to him had called it the Desert Eagle of China. Top-shelf quality. Rock-bottom price. Superb stopping power. Two hundred dollars had sealed the deal.

But now, thinking back, he wondered if he had been too hasty. Perhaps he could have haggled for a lower price. Perhaps. But, ah, what did it matter now? He had his weapon, and it would serve its purpose.

Reaching into his bag once more, he drew out an ammunition magazine. It held seven rounds. Remembering what the seller had taught him, he checked the gun's safety catch, making sure it was secure. Then he tilted the gun to one side, lining up the magazine with the bottom of the handgrip, slotting it in smoothly until it locked into place. Finally, holding the gun straight, he reached for the slide above the barrel. Pulling it, he chambered a round with a satisfying click-clack. Oh yes. He had to admit that the sound gave him a small thrill. Made him feel like a real soldier.

Soldier.

He relished the word.

Retrieving another magazine from his bag, he slipped it into his jacket's left pocket, while the gun went into the right. That gave him a total of fourteen rounds to play with. *Inshallah*, it would be enough.

Samir bowed his head. '*Bismillah ir-Rahman ir-Rahim...*' In the name of God, the Compassionate, the Merciful. He recited the eighty-seventh *surah*, a favourite of the Holy Prophet. 'Success comes to him who grows, who remembers the name of his Lord, who performs his prayer. It is better to forsake the ways of the world, for heaven is everlasting. Yes, this is inscribed in the scrolls of the ancients...'

Samir nodded, inhaling deeply.

His migraine had dimmed to an insignificant throb.

Alhamdulillah.

He was ready.

Pulling his jacket's hood over his head, he pushed his car door open, stepping out on to the sidewalk. A puddle splashed under his shoe. Raindrops prickled his face. He shut his door and locked it.

That's when footsteps came up behind him. He froze, and adrenaline spiked in his stomach. Had he been discovered? Had someone called the police on him? Shaking, he fumbled for the gun in his pocket, his thumb finding the safety. All he had to do was flick it off and the gun would be ready to fire. And he whirled, ready to unleash hell. But – *damn it* – it was just a woman with an umbrella walking her dog. Twisting his lips, feeling foolish, he swallowed the knot in his throat and relaxed his grip on his gun, but not by much.

The dog sniffed at him, its tongue lolling and dripping saliva, and he backed up against the side of his car. He didn't know what breed it was. Didn't care. The imam at his mosque had warned him about the uncleanliness of dogs. Yes, they were useful for guarding and hunting. But as pets? Playthings? Never. It was *haram* – forbidden.

The woman smiled at Samir. But he just stared. Yes, he could kill her right now if he wanted to – her and her filthy dog. Stroking the curve of his gun's trigger, he allowed the fantasy to linger, watching as they rounded the corner. When they were gone, he shook his head and exhaled. He had been so close – too close – to losing control.

God is challenging you. Placing obstacles in your path. Seeing if you are worthy. But… of course you are worthy. You will not deviate from the path. You will not falter. Your heart is pure. Your faith is strong. Your cause is just.

Samir shook his head harder and crossed the street.

The house was one of the prettiest in the neighbourhood. A large two-storey, it sat last on the block, shaded by a willowy tree, its lawn decorated by bonsai shrubs, flower beds and a bubbling fish pond. A short white fence completed its charm. Made it picture perfect. Like a postcard image. More than anything, Samir wished it would burn. All of it.

He approached the house from the back, his eyes darting to make sure he was alone. Nervous energy pulsed through him, warm and dizzying. His body tensed, like a spring coiled up to its tightest.

Do it. Just do it. Do not hesitate. Never hesitate.

He broke into a running start, jumping the fence, clearing it, the breeze tousling his hood. But his landing on the other side was clumsy. He slipped on the wet lawn, the soles of his shoes squeaking, and he dropped to his knees, skidding as he did, the freshly cut grass loose, its earthy smell tickling his nostrils.

Jerking his head this way and that way, he panted, his heart thundering. Had someone heard him? Curses. He almost lost his nerve. Almost clambered back over the fence. Almost ran away. But – *no* – he crossed his arms over his chest and clutched himself tight. Head bowed, he whispered rapid-fire verses about courage and fortitude and self-belief and staying the course.

Restrain your fear. God is with you. God is always with you. Do not deviate from the path. Not now. Not when you are so close. For it is not your will that matters. It is God's will. Always God's will.

Slowly, surely, his panic eased, and when Samir looked up, he realised that nothing had stirred around him. No lights came on. No footsteps approached. No one shouted. Nothing. He was safe.

Alhamdulillah.

God had preserved him despite his clumsiness.

Alhamdulillah.

He started to move. Keeping himself low, he inched towards the pond. Colourful fish darted as he drew close.

Curious, he dipped his fingers into the bubbling water. It was warm. Artificially heated. He scoffed. How could it be that the apostate treated his fish better than he treated his own people?

In his mind's eye, Samir remembered something he had seen in the news – a *kafir* helicopter strafing and rocketing a Muslim home, turning it into smouldering rubble. Heinous. Yet, as bad as the *kuffar* were, the apostate was worse. Much worse. For he had chosen to side with them.

Traitor.

Seething, Samir felt his way around the circumference of the pond and found wires. He followed them, and they led him straight to the power socket. He tore off its plastic cover and yanked the electrical plug loose. The water stopped bubbling. Good. The fish could freeze for all he cared.

He turned his attention to the smooth rocks decorating the edge of the pond. Picking up one as big as his palm, he weighed it in his hand. Too small. Too light.

Dropping it, he chose another rock, this one as large as his fist. He had to stretch his fingers to grip it. Yes, this one would do nicely.

Cradling the rock against his chest, he drew his gun. He looked past the patio, past the deck chairs, past the potted plants. Finally his eyes settled on the glass door that led to the living room.

He thought of his children, Abu and Fatimah. Still so young. Still so innocent. He hoped they would understand. He hoped they would be proud. And with that, he thumbed his gun's safety catch off.

2

Abraham Khan had just sat down for dinner when his wife gasped. He frowned and lowered his fork to his plate. Following her gaze, he looked out the windows.

Belinda pointed shakily. 'There's someone in the garden.'

'Are you sure?'

'Yes.'

Abraham pushed his chair back and stood. Craning his neck, he swept his eyes over the fish pond. The flower beds. The shrubs. The fence line. But all he saw were their plants swaying in the drizzling twilight.

Eventually, he shook his head. 'I don't see anything.'

'Abe, I'm telling you, there's a man outside.'

Abraham reached for a switch on the wall, flipping on the spotlights. They blazed to life, blanketing the yard in a warm glow, chasing away all the shadows. He gave everything another look. Nothing. No bogeyman anywhere.

He turned back to his wife, agitation creeping into his voice. 'There's no one there.'

'We should call the police anyway.'

'We are not going to call the police every time you imagine a prowler.'

Belinda scrunched up her face. 'I didn't imagine it!'

Abraham wanted to snap back, but he dug his fingernails into his palms instead. They had been on edge for two months now. It had started with phone calls threatening obscenities, then dog shit stuffed into their mailbox, red paint splashed on their bonsai shrubs, arsenic dumped into their fish pond.

Eventually, the police had arrested the boy and the girl responsible – religious nuts who had taken things too far. That should have been the end of the matter. But not for Belinda. She had remained a nervous wreck ever since. Always jumping at shadows. She just couldn't shake the feeling that there were more crazies out there. Watching. Waiting.

Abraham forced himself to smile, but it felt more like a grimace. 'The rain and the wind are playing tricks on your eyes. You have to let it go.'

Belinda gazed down at her plate. 'I can't.'

'Try, darling.'

'Don't you know how scared I am?'

Belinda blinked back tears. She looked so small right then. So vulnerable.

Abraham regretted his tone. It wasn't like them to get angry with each other. It wasn't like them at all. Softening, he reached out to touch her, to comfort her. 'I'm sorry—'

That's when the glass door in the lounge behind them exploded. Fragments shrieked, peppering the floor.

Abraham froze in mid-step.

Belinda clutched her mouth.

A hooded intruder loomed on the patio just outside, smashing away at the glass frame with a rock before plunging his arm through, reaching for the door handle.

Abraham stared with his eyes wide, unable to move, unable to breathe, unable to comprehend, panic shutting down his brain, paralysing his limbs. Everything was happening in slow motion. But then Belinda's scream jolted him, and he snapped out of his stupor.

He knew they had to get upstairs.

Damn it, their only chance was to get upstairs.

So he caught Belinda's arm, pulling her to her feet, her chair toppling, and he spun her around, pushing her towards the staircase, urging her to run like the wind.

Dear God...

The intruder was already through the door, his shoes crunching on broken glass, his voice booming, calling Abraham a blasphemer, calling for him to die.

Belinda hit the stairs with her legs pumping, surging ahead, taking two steps at a time, and that's when Abraham heard a click. It was an ominous click, a terrifying click, like a gun's hammer being cocked.

Fear squeezed his throat shut.

God Almighty.

He choked, wishing he could move faster and wasn't stuck in slow motion. He could feel an icy spot building right at the back of his skull as if a bullet was going to smash into him at any second and blow his head apart.

3

Hot tears spilled from Samir's eyes, streaking his cheeks. 'Blasphemer! Blasphemer! You must die!'

He remembered the oppressed *ummah*, the brotherhood of believers around the world, and swearing he'd strike a blow for them all, he pulled back his pistol's hammer, aiming it one-handed. At last – *at last* – he had the apostate in his sights, and this was the moment of moments, his moment of moments, and he knew he was an instrument of the divine.

'La ilaha illa Allah.' There is no god but God.

Samir squeezed the trigger, and the pistol roared and kicked, its power making his blood rush, causing him to stagger back two steps, gunpowder scorching his nostrils.

Up on the staircase, the wall beside the apostate's head exploded, white plaster misting the air. The apostate lurched, and his wife screamed.

Samir recovered his footing, realising he had used the wrong grip, the wrong stance, and that he'd been hasty, much too hasty. So he lined up another shot, this time clutching his gun with both hands, locking his elbows, vowing he would not miss because the apostate was already at the top of the stairs, already darting into the hallway beyond.

Samir squeezed the trigger, and it clicked, not firing.

Confused, he squeezed it again and again.

No. No. No.

Not now.

Not when he was so close.

He smacked his palm against the gun, racking the slide back, trying to clear the jam, a round ejecting, flipping, arching. He squeezed the trigger again, and it still wouldn't work, and he racked the slide again, ejecting another round, squeezing again, but still nothing.

What to do?

What to do?

Damn it. Damn it. Damn it.

Hurling the gun, sending it crashing against the dinner table, dishes clattering, he stormed the stairs, his heart thudding in his ears, knowing he would have to kill the apostate with his bare hands.

In between breaths, he stuttered a prayer, *'Bismillah ir-Rahman ir-Rahim...'* In the name of God, the Compassionate, the Merciful.

He had almost reached the top when he stubbed his foot on the lip of a step, clumsy, so clumsy, and he twisted his ankle and fell, cracking his head against the staircase's railing. White-hot pain flowered in his skull, and his hair felt wet and sticky, and curses, he was bleeding all over.

Gasping, shaking, he picked himself up and limped into the hallway, a door slamming ahead of him, and he could hear screeching and thumping on the other side. It sounded like the apostate and his wife were shifting furniture against the door, barricading it.

4

Belinda Freeman-Khan sobbed and screamed herself raw.

Hot, bitter vomit climbed up the back of her throat, scorching her senses, and she couldn't breathe, couldn't think, and the room around her seemed to warp and blacken and spin. Her knees almost buckled, and she wanted nothing better than to collapse and curl up into the smallest, tightest ball and pass out and hope against hope that this wasn't happening and—

Dear God.

She doubled over and vomited, her insides churning, cramping.

Her husband was behind the dressing table now, his face stricken as he grunted and heaved and pushed. He was yelling at her to get up, to help him, to stay strong.

Belinda stumbled over, still puking as she went, and together, side by side, they pushed and pushed. But the table was heavy as hell and kept getting caught up in the carpet, creaking, jerking, her jewellery falling, her cosmetics falling, all her precious things falling. But she didn't care, couldn't care, because all she wanted to do was to keep the bad man away, and they had to hurry because he was coming, definitely coming.

They managed to shove the table against the door, and that's when the bad man crashed against it with a terrible bang.

Belinda yelped, slipping, falling, and she scooted backwards, the carpet searing her butt through her skirt, her hands covering her face. Suddenly she found herself hating Abe for being so stubborn, so naive, so blind, refusing to face up to the danger all these months, all these damn months, and now it was too late, much too late.

Peering through the gaps between her fingers, Belinda caught her husband scrambling this way and that way around the bed, straining and panting as he tried to shift it. The sight of him made her stomach turn, and she gagged, feeling the urge to vomit, but she was all spent and thirsty as hell, and there was nothing left to vomit.

Oh God.

No, she didn't hate Abe.

How could she hate him?

She loved him.

Damn it, she loved him despite it all.

Quitting her self-pity, Belinda rose and got beside him even though her limbs were numb, so terribly numb, feeling as if they weren't hers anymore. But – *screw it* – she shook her head, snivelling, forcing away the blackness squeezing in on her consciousness, and inch by excruciating inch, with the bed groaning as it shifted, she pushed and stumbled, pushed and stumbled, her muscles burning, her lungs screaming.

Her mind was on autopilot, no longer thinking, just fighting to survive, just fighting to survive because – *damn it* – she wasn't ready to die just yet.

5

Samir hurled himself against the door, crying out with each impact, determined to overpower them with his righteousness. But, curses, they had wedged something larger and heavier against the door, and no matter how hard he tried, it wouldn't budge.

It was no use, no use at all, and curses, he would have to find another way, so he sagged against the wall, lurched back towards the staircase. He descended, retching and coughing and spitting out bloody saliva, the pain in his skull throbbing, his vision growing fuzzy, his spirit wavering.

No, no, no. Do not doubt now. Do not despair. This is a test of faith. A test of commitment. God is watching you. Always watching you. The Compassionate. The Merciful. The Gracious. The Evolver. The Fashioner of Forms. This is jihad. You cannot falter now. You must not falter now.

Clutching his head, Samir found the kitchen and made for the stove and started fiddling with its knobs, half-crying, half-laughing. Yes, he would use fire, cleansing fire, to destroy the entire house. He would be a *shahid*, a martyr, the greatest of honours. Oh, how much he ached to be a *shahid* like the great

Osama bin Laden, to avenge the Holy Prophet, to be rewarded with paradise, to make his family proud and—

That's when Samir blinked and saw that the stove was electric, not gas.

He howled.

Why, God, why?

Mad with rage, he swept his arm across the dish rack, plates flipping, shattering. He tore out drawer after drawer, cabinet after cabinet, scattering their contents, breaking out in feverish sweat.

He launched himself against the fridge, rocking it back and forth until it toppled, bursting open. He was delirious, oh so delirious, and he didn't hear the sirens, the footsteps, the voices until the two police officers were right on top of him, screaming, their tasers drawn.

'On your knees now! On your knees!'

'Comply! Comply!'

Panting, Samir picked up a meat cleaver. He raised it above his head, and he charged them. *'Allahu akbar!'* God is great!

The officers fired their tasers.

There was a whoosh of air and a hissing sound.

Samir felt a stinging sensation in his chest, and it swelled into a wave of numbness and nausea. A thousand volts of electricity rocked him, and he slumped to the floor, convulsing. The last thing he felt before his consciousness winked out was his arms being forced behind his back and handcuffs biting into his wrists.

Samir gasped.

Oh, my Prophet, my Prophet. I have failed you.

PART TWO

6

'Good morning. If you've just joined us, you're listening to Tough Talk. I'm Hayley Ngata. Today I have a special guest with me here in the studio. Reverend Jonah Vosen probably needs no introduction. He is the founder and director of the Ascension Group, a think tank and advocacy foundation based on Christian values. No stranger to controversy, he is well-known for his biting social commentary. But love him or hate him, you have to agree that he's always an interesting man to talk to. Reverend, thank you for being here, and welcome to our programme.'

'Gidday, Hayley. Hello, everyone.'

'Reverend, as we all know, Abraham Khan and his wife were attacked last night by an armed intruder. The nation is shocked, and it's put us all on edge. What are your thoughts?'

'First, let me just say that I'm thankful that Mr and Mrs Khan are safe. I can only imagine how traumatised they must be. What they have gone through is appalling. I am praying that they find strength during this very difficult time.'

'Even though Mr Khan is a Muslim and his wife is agnostic?'

'I pray for them anyway. I don't discriminate.'

'Good on you, Reverend. Now, regarding the incident itself...'

'Shocking, yes, but hardly surprising. This has happened because we have allowed undesirable cultures to take root in this country.'

'You are referring to Mr Khan?'

'No, Hayley. Goodness, no. I'm talking in general here. For instance, let's take the radical who tried to murder Mr Khan. His name, I believe, is—'

'Um, I'm sorry, but I'm going to have to stop you there. My producer's in my ear, telling me that the suspect has been granted legal name suppression. We can't allow his name to be broadcast.'

'My mistake. I apologise. Well, let me put it to you another way. Most immigrants arrive on our shores with a genuine desire to contribute to our beautiful land. To add to our diversity. But it appears that some are failing to assimilate. They are either unwilling or incapable.'

'Reverend, isn't that racist?'

'I beg your pardon?'

'Well, the prime minister has called you a far-right xenophobe. She's attacked you as being out of step with modern, multicultural New Zealand. And many Christian and Muslim leaders agree. They accuse you of perpetuating a separatist cult.'

'Come on, Hayley. That's a weak argument, and you know it. I have Dutch, Welsh and Maori blood running through my veins. I do understand the value of multiculturalism. In fact, I celebrate it. But at the same time, I'm also a pragmatist. By any chance, have you read Samuel Huntington's Clash of Civilizations?'

'No, I can't say I have. But I do know that it's been cited a lot since September 11th. Something about cultural fault lines...'

'That's right, Hayley. Fault lines. Flashpoints. Mismatched cultures in violent collision. Everything else is just icing on the cake.'

'Icing on the cake?'

'Here's an example. Saudi Arabia is the largest exporter of oil; the United States is the largest importer of oil. And guess what? Fifteen of the nineteen hijackers on 9/11 were Saudis.'

'Yeah. Okay.'

'Consider that for a moment. Why would Saudi citizens attack America? Their single biggest customer? Does it make sense? Does it add up?'

'No, I have to admit it doesn't.'

'You see, it's not a traditional conflict over resource or territory that we are witnessing. It's really a conflict over hearts and minds. A cultural conflict. A conflict that you and I aren't even aware of until it creeps up on us and explodes in our faces. That's what so many fail to understand.'

'So you're against... what? Muslim immigrants?'

'Just those who seek to take us back to the seventh century.'

'Extremists, then.'

'Yes, extremists. Radicals. Jihadists.'

'Reverend, if you don't mind me saying, you're pretty radical yourself. Isn't it hypocritical and unfair to be singling out Muslims and dumping it all on them?'

'I'm not discriminating against any one religion.'

'Yet you seem to be drawing a direct link between Muslims and violence.'

'Will you allow me to put it all into context?'

'Sure. Go ahead.'

'Okay. You're familiar with how critics make fun of my faith and the things I hold absolutely sacred. Does that justify me going out and murdering them? Wrecking violent vengeance upon them? Of course not. Yes, their comments may cause me outrage. But I must still tolerate their right to say what they want to say. It is the rule of law. It is the cornerstone of who we are as a society. So, to be clear, I'm only against those who reject freedom of speech in favour of barbarism.'

'But shouldn't free speech have its limits? I mean, insensitive portrayals of Prophet Muhammad have hurt Muslim sensibilities in the past, and we've seen the consequences of that overseas. Should we allow free speech to run amok when we know what it will lead to?'

'Hayley, the freedom that gives naysayers the right to insult God is the same freedom that gives me the right to share my faith. It works both ways. It's how a mature and dynamic society works. Now, we may not always agree with one another. But we can at least accommodate dissenting opinions. Censorship is not the answer. As a journalist, you would know that.'

'So you are in favour of Mr Khan pushing ahead with his book tour.'

'Indeed, I am. Mr Khan is a good Muslim and a good citizen. I have the highest respect for what he's trying to achieve. He is not intimidated by terrorists, nor should he be. He represents a new breed of Muslim progressives. Someone who uses literature to inspire intellectual advancement instead of blowing himself up to make a point. Now, small as our country may be, it has always stood up for what's right at critical moments in history. This happens to be one of them. We have an obligation to support and protect Mr Khan as he embarks on his mission.'

'And you stand by that even if he inspires outbreaks of violence?

'That's actually a moot point. We knew the risks when we gave him asylum here. We knew how much those fascists in the Muslim world hated him. But as the old saying goes, the enemy of my enemy is my friend. So we can't back down. Not now. Not ever. '

7

'So you think you can fight?' Maya Raines eyed the students before her.

They were fit and trim and confident. The kind of girls who knew their place in the world and weren't afraid to show it.

One of them raised her hand. 'Miss Raines?'

Maya nodded. 'Yes, Zoe?'

'We're, like, black belts. We know all about fighting.'

The group sniggered. Lots of *oohs* and *ahhs*.

'So you wouldn't be afraid if some street punk tried to rape you?'

Zoe rolled her eyes. 'Afraid? I would kick his ass.'

The group laughed. The *oohs* and *ahhs* got louder.

Maya folded her arms, trying her damndest to keep a straight face. It didn't help that the community hall they were in actually doubled as a children's playgroup on weekdays. Cutesy drawings and craftwork decorated the walls. No, not exactly favourable to creating fear. If she had her way, she would have held this lesson in a dark and damp alleyway past midnight. Not a cutesy community hall on a Saturday morning.

Still, she didn't see it as a negative. Sure, the young ladies were cocky now. But once the right stimulus was applied, fear would flow naturally.

Maya waited for the laughter to die down before speaking up, 'Zoe, if you don't mind me asking, what's your discipline?'

'Tae kwon do.'

'And your rank?'

'Second *dan*.'

'Right. So you can handle yourself – you can kick fast, and you can kick hard.'

'Yeah.'

'Do you want to put that to the test?'

'Hell, yeah.'

The group parted and Zoe stepped forward, bold as a peacock.

Maya took hold of the whistle hanging from her neck and raised it to her lips. She blew it long and hard, its shrill blast echoing throughout the hall.

A door at the other end opened.

A man emerged, wrapped up in safety pads and wearing an enormous silver helmet that masked his face. He looked like a lumbering alien as he moved towards them, shifting his weight from side to side.

Zoe stared as the man stopped in front of her, stretching his gloved hands, his joints popping. The students murmured among themselves.

Maya clapped to get their attention. 'Girls, meet Bulletman. You can think of him as being a crash-test dummy on steroids. The rules are simple. Zoe? Pay attention, Zoe. You're going to try and get past him. And Bulletman? Well, he's going to try and block you. You can hit him as hard as you want, anywhere you want. Head, groin, legs, whatever – it's all fair game. And don't you worry about the helmet. It's padded with four layers. You won't hurt yourself by attacking it. Now, bear in mind, Bulletman won't be hitting back, but he will be pushing. He'll be pushing hard. Any questions?'

Zoe raised her hand. 'Miss Raines? Don't I get to wear, like, protective gear?'

Maya smiled. 'Protective gear is for wimps like Bulletman, not a tough cookie like you. Besides, the floor is padded. That's all you really need. Cool?'

'Oh. Cool.' Zoe entered a sparring stance, arms raised, fists clenched as she bounced up and down, puffing fiercely.

A bad start, Maya knew. The bouncing would only compromise her centre of gravity, while the puffing would over-pressurise her blood, wrecking all muscle control. The worst possible combination.

Maya blew the whistle, and Bulletman rushed Zoe with all the force of a freight train, screaming, 'You think you can get past me, bitch? You think you can? I'm going to beat the shit out of you! I'm going to break your pretty face!'

Zoe spun and kicked, but it was too weak, too hasty, and she missed. Bulletman walloped into her, shoving her back, and she drifted to the left, gasping, punching – *one, two, three* – but they were glancing blows, feeble, ineffective.

Bulletman crashed into her once more, and this time she drifted to the right, bouncing, kicking – *one, two* – but Bulletman gave her no room, and he powered his head into her, destroying her centre of gravity.

Suddenly she was retreating, staggering, tripping, no more conviction, no more technique. Her eyes were dazed, her face pinched, her body looking like a puppet flailing on invisible strings as Bulletman screamed and pushed, screamed and pushed, screamed and pushed.

She finally went down, scrambling against the wall, squeezing herself into a pitiful ball, Bulletman hovering over her, banging his fists, growling.

Maya checked her watch.

Ten seconds.

Yeah, things had gone far enough.

She blew the whistle.

Bulletman ceased his assault and stepped away.

Slowly, Zoe uncurled herself, her chest heaving, her face red as a cherry. The salty smell of sweat hung thick in the air. The smell of fear.

No one moved.

No one spoke.

Eventually, Bulletman reached for Zoe and helped her to her feet.

Maya allowed the silence to linger for a bit before breaking it, 'What you've just seen is called the adrenaline dump. Let me just say that again: adrenaline dump. Your heart races. Your vision tunnels. You start to shake. You can't breathe. You lose fine motor control. Your reflexes go wonky. Time slows down. You lose focus. Your black belt doesn't help you. You forget all your fancy moves. You get overwhelmed. You get pummelled. You get raped. You become a statistic. End of story.'

Maya walked to a bench nearby and unclasped the chilly bin sitting on it. Icy vapour swirled as she got out a sports drink. Cracking the can open with a fizz, Maya handed it to Bulletman, who handed it to Zoe.

Zoe accepted the drink with shivering hands, her head bowed.

Maya turned back to the students.

Their faces were pale.

They didn't look so smug now.

'Girls, there's the *dojo* and then there's the streets. Chances are, your instructors have never been in real confrontation on the streets. They don't even know what it feels like. They can't tell you about the hormones pumping through your blood, the neurons firing in your brain, the spasms attacking your muscles. They can't coach you what to do when your reptilian side overpowers your mammalian side. I mean, we are so used to thinking of ourselves as civilised and restrained human beings that we have completely lost touch with the very instincts that are vital for keeping us alive and well. That's what this course is meant to fix. I want my students to understand the adrenaline dump. I want them to master it. Because, girls, you already have the tools. Evolutionary biology is hiding in plain sight. Don't believe me? Then spread your fingers. Go ahead. Lift up your hands and spread your fingers. Notice the webbed skin between them? There you go. Your reptilian roots are right there, buried beneath a mammalian façade. Now, if you can use that under stress, under extreme stress, it might just prove to be the difference.'

Maya studied the group. They looked lost, as if she had just been speaking to them in Latin. Obviously, she needed to unblock their minds with a hard and fast demonstration. Nodding at Bulletman, she took off her whistle and her cell phone and placed them on the bench.

Maya turned just as Bulletman rushed forward, screaming, 'You damn bitch! I'm gonna kill you! I'm gonna kill you!'

Maya felt the adrenaline ribbon through her like an explosion of warmth, pitching her to the edge, causing her to see red. Her body shook like she was being caught up in a hurricane, but she forced herself to breathe in through the nose, out through the mouth. She was conscious of her thundering heartbeat, welcoming the rush, riding it, allowing her raw primal instincts to take over.

Maya juked right, forcing Bulletman to shift his momentum to chase her, and then she danced back to the left. She slammed the web between her forefinger and thumb into his throat, hearing him grunt, stopping him in mid-lunge. Then she palm-struck his face in a blur – *bam, bam, bam*. The force came from deep within her, the very core of her being, as she turned fear into rage, her screams eclipsing his as she refused to back down, refused to be a victim.

Staggering now, Bulletman shoved her back and swung his arms wildly, delivering jabs, crosses, hooks. But Maya simply dodged his punches, keeping herself out of range, allowing him to tire himself out.

She weaved left, then right, hitting him with a low kick to the kneecap, then another to the groin, and as he stumbled, she closed in, slipping through his weakened defences. She blocked his feeble punches, then hit him with jabs of her own, finishing up with an elbow strike to the face.

Now the tide of the battle had well and truly turned, and as Bulletman faltered, Maya hooked one leg behind his, tripping him. They went down together, thumping hard on the mat. She was on top of him now, pummelling his face with palm strikes – *one, two, three, four*.

He jerked like a wild bull and threw her off, but she readjusted her position and scissored her legs around his torso and neck. At the same time, she grabbed his arm and stretched it out, hyperextending the joint, locking him down.

Bulletman groaned and convulsed.

But there was no escape.

Eventually he tapped his free hand against the mat, conceding defeat.

Maya paused for dramatic effect. Then, slowly, very slowly, she released the armbar and disengaged from the grapple.

She rose to her feet. Her tunnelled senses eased as she came down from the adrenaline high, and she became aware of the students clapping and cheering and whooping as they crowded around her with Zoe at the forefront, wide-eyed and eager.

'That's way awesome!'

'Unreal! Never seen anything like it!'

'You were like an animal, Miss Raines! Like an animal!'

Maya could do little but pant and smile. That's when her cell phone buzzed on the bench, cutting short the kudos.

Zoe scooped it up and handed it over. 'Here you go, Miss Raines.'

'Cheers.'

Maya checked the caller ID.

It was Deirdre Raines.

Mama.

She sighed, and her smile became a frown. Shaking her head, she straightened. 'Girls, I'm so sorry, but I'm going to have to cut this short. That's it for today's introductory session. Bulletman – also known as Eli – will be taking down your details if you are keen to sign up for the full course. Thank you. Have a good day.'

Maya turned away from the chattering girls.

Mama.

They hadn't spoken to each other since that night. They had gotten in each other's faces back then, arguing, neither of them backing down, and in the end, Maya had left, vowing never to return.

She flexed her fingers around her phone. The hurt was still raw, jabbing and twisting in her like fish hooks.

Mama, you're choosing a lousy time to call.

She made for the community hall's entrance and pushed the door open. The autumn breeze tousled her hair. Dry leaves skittered along in the parking lot. The sky was gunmetal grey.

Maya answered her phone. 'Yes?'

Mama's voice was flat and cold. 'Maya, I'm putting you on assignment.'

'I can't do it. Sorry.'

Mama ignored her. 'Our principal is Abraham Khan. It's all over the news, so I'm sure you're aware that an attempt was made on him last night.'

'You'll have to find someone else—'

'The police have relocated him to the Pacifica Hotel, and there is every chance that this thing might escalate.'

'Please find someone else—'

'The Diplomatic Protection Squad is up to their eyeballs with the economic summit in Wellington. They cannot redeploy to Auckland. Not for the next few days. So, for now, Section One is being tapped to look after Khan.'

Maya sighed. 'I'm not in the right state of mind.'

'I'm not playing your games, Maya. Not today. Dashiell and Arthur are already on-site. Noah will be at your place in an hour. That's final.'

'Mama—'

'I said that's final. Just do your job.'

Maya frowned as the line disconnected with a click. She felt her stomach clench up, and her mouth tasted sour.

Yes, Mama was doing what she did best.

Being a dragon lady.

Never taking no for an answer.

IF YOU HAVE ENJOYED
READING THIS EXCERPT
FROM *THE BLASPHEMER*,
YOU CAN PURCHASE THE
BOOK NOW AT ALL ONLINE
RETAILERS.

ABOUT THE AUTHOR

John Ling is the author of international thrillers that have appeared on the USA Today and Amazon bestseller lists.

He was born into an ethnic Chinese family and raised as a Christian in Muslim-majority Malaysia. He now lives in New Zealand. His exotic cultural background, straddling East and West, informs his storytelling.

Visit his website at johnling.net

Made in the USA
Columbia, SC
06 January 2018